THE CEMETERY CLUB

ISBN: 978-1-940222-83-7
First Edition
Printed in the USA

Cover and interior design by Kelsey Rice

THE
CEMETERY
CLUB

A DARCY & FLORA COZY MYSTERY

BLANCHE DAY MANOS
& BARBARA BURGESS

P
Pen-L Publishing
Fayetteville, AR
Pen-L.com

Dedication

BLANCHE DAY MANOS: *The Cemetery Club* is dedicated to my son, Matt Manos and to my mother, Susie Latty Day. These two always encouraged and inspired me. Co-author Barbara Burgess and I also want to credit the memory of our mutual friend, Levern Jones, who introduced us and so set the wheels of this book in motion.

CHAPTER 1

When I awoke to sunshine, blue skies, and the fragrance of freshly-perked coffee that morning, I had no inkling that a few hours later the sun would be blotted out by menacing clouds or that my mother and I would stumble upon a dead body in a brush pile in Goshen Cemetery. Mom's purpose in coming to the cemetery was to see what needed to be done before Decoration Day, which would happen on the third Sunday of this month of May. My purpose was simply to be with her.

But there it was—a bare human foot sticking stiffly from a mound of dirt and tree limbs heaped in the oldest part of the ancient graveyard called Goshen. Nature itself seemed to recoil at the horror before us. Trees bowed and swayed in a macabre dance with the wild wind while angry clouds brooded over the gray headstones. I had seen more than one dead body in my years as an investigative reporter, but this shocked me to the core because it was so unexpected and horrible.

Mom grabbed my arm. "Darcy," she said, "is that what I think it is?"

I swallowed before I could answer. "I'm afraid so."

"But—but, how can that be?" Mom's voice quavered. "Who is it? Come on, let's uncover him. Maybe he is alive. Maybe we can help." She started toward the pile of debris.

I grabbed her hand. "No. Don't go there. We need to get the sheriff. Whoever is under that brush is beyond all help."

Flora Tucker did not take advice easily. She pulled away from me and made a beeline for the grisly object. Past examples of her courage flashed through my mind: Mom gently carrying me to the doctor when, as a child, I fell from a tree and broke my arm; another time, she loaded Dad's old rifle and poked around the foundation of our barn until she found and shot the copperhead that bit my father. She was not a large woman, but she had a lot of grit.

Nevertheless, I tried to stop her. "You shouldn't see what's under there," I pleaded. "Think about it, Mom. This is a job for the authorities."

She shook off my hand as if I were a pesky mosquito, grabbed a stick from that pile of trash, and began scooting away the limbs and rocks until she uncovered a green plaid shirt. Removing a few more sticks revealed arms folded across a man's chest and just a few inches under his arms gaped a ragged, dark bullet hole. Another two seconds of digging and the dead man's face appeared. He had a dark complexion and longish gray hair.

Mom gasped and shuddered like the limbs of the surrounding cedars. "It—it's Ben," she whispered.

I held my nose and leaned forward. She was right. Ben Ventris, a longtime neighbor of Mom and Dad's, lay before me. I had visited in the Ventris home many years ago when Mrs. Ventris was alive. I remembered a comfortable house and the scent of wood smoke. Their farm connected to land owned by my grandmother. But now, here was Ben, still and lifeless, thrown away like someone's trash. Tears stung my eyes.

Something else about Ben Ventris did not look right, besides the fact that he was quite dead. Mom noticed it at the same time as I. Her hand on my arm felt like a vise. "Look!" she whispered hoarsely. "Oh, dear Lord, Darcy, look at Ben's poor hand."

I looked. Only a bloody stump remained where the third finger of Ben's left hand should have been. Nausea welled up in my throat and I heard my mother gag.

"Somebody cut off Ben's finger," Mom whispered.

As we stood, mesmerized by the horror in front of us, a strange silence descended on the graveyard. I raised my head to see what was happening. Dark clouds that had brooded above us now moved and churned and a small eddy of whirling air pointed downward. My heart stopped, then thudded against my ribs.

"That's a tornado!" I yelled. "If it drops, we are in trouble!"

As if in agreement, a low roar began over our heads and wind, hail, and rain came at us, battling to whirl us into the seething heavens.

Mom and I linked arms and stumbled into the storm. Putting her mouth close to my ear, she shouted, "The chapel!"

We struggled toward a small, sandstone building at the edge of Goshen Cemetery. Rain blinded us, hail pelted us, and tree branches flew past, but at last we reached the little building. I tugged the door open and we both fell inside, gulping blessedly dry air.

Mom sank into a pew and I leaned against the wall. The storm's roar dimmed to a comparative quiet within this sanctuary. I was about to sit beside my mother when I heard a sharp click and felt a breeze eddy around me. A shiver traced its way down my spine. Had the back door of the chapel just opened and closed?

"Who's there?" I called.

"I don't care who it was," Mom said, her teeth chattering. "Maybe someone else wanted out of the storm. At the moment, I'd share space with Mick Monroney himself."

While I doubted that it was Ventris County's notorious outlaw from the 1930s who had gone out of the door, I could not see much in the dim room. I flipped the light switch. Nothing happened. Evidently, the electric power was a victim of the storm.

Turning the lock in the front door, I felt my way through murky semi-darkness to the other end of the building. No shadowy figure lurked anywhere that I could see. Our arrival must have sent someone who had sheltered here into the storm. Groping for the bolt on the door, I slid it into place, and fumbled my way back to the pew where Mom huddled.

"I wish I had a jacket to put around you," I said. "You must be chilled to the bone."

"I'll be all right," she said. "It's the shock of finding Ben more than being cold. Do you have your cell phone?"

Of course! Why hadn't I thought of that handy little electronic gadget? Delving into my purse, I found it and flipped it open. I punched in 911. Nothing lit up nor buzzed nor played music. I shook my head.

"No signal. We must be out of range."

Mom sighed. "There are lots of hills around. That must be the reason. This storm will let up sooner or later and then we can get safely back home."

Getting safely back home, I feared, might not be so easy. Wind pounded the chapel and did its best to come in the door or through the roof. Lightning flashes lit up row after row of wood benches inside our shelter. Thankfully, the benches had no other occupants. An old, upright piano crouched in a shadowy corner, and a small table with a lectern on top stood in front of the pews. My ancestors had gathered here in this small cemetery for countless funerals and Decoration Days. Mom's grandfather helped build the chapel. Through the years, Goshen had been a place to worship and for mourners to hear the comforting Word of God when burying a loved one. However, after this traumatic day, Goshen Cemetery would never be the same for me. Something more dreadful and violent than a spring storm had happened here. A good man's life had been cut short, wrested violently from him by an unknown assassin.

"We need to pray, Darcy," Mom said softly. I nodded. Together, we began Psalm 91, the Protection Psalm. "*He that dwelleth in the secret place of the most High shall abide under the shadow of the Almighty.*"

Mom and I needed the assurance that God was with us. I once fully believed this, but events of the last few months had done nothing to strengthen my faith. When my husband Jake died, the ground shifted under my feet. My rock was gone. Why had God allowed Jake to die? Did He care that I was suffering as I had never suffered before? How could it be His will to cut short the life of one as honest and kind and loving as my husband? Of course, I knew that Jake was in heaven, but what about me? I was left to carry on somehow without him, and I sorely missed Jake Campbell's strong arms around me.

Returning to Levi, Oklahoma, the place of my birth, yesterday gave me the eerie feeling that I had never left. I came home seeking healing, hoping that being away from the Dallas house that I had shared with Jake would somehow ease the aching loneliness. Since that awful morning when I awoke in our bed and found that a heart attack had stolen my husband, I had lived with emptiness. Moving through each nightmarish day, I pretended that Jake was in the next room or had just gone downtown. At other times, the cold fact that my husband would never return hit me full force and I knew that, somehow, I would have to carry on without him. During the weeks after Jake's funeral, I wandered through the house, wondering what to do with it and all the furnishings, unable to concentrate on my job at *The Dallas Morning News*, even though the editor told me I could work from home. I still had an unfinished assignment for the paper which was nowhere nearly completed. Thankfully, Jake's life insurance was enough so that I could take time off from my job without financial worry.

Mom wanted me to come live with her. She was lonely too, although Dad had died twenty years before. So, when my house sold, I loaded up my personal belongings and headed back to Levi, hoping some of my mother's courage would rub off on me.

A brilliant flash, a roar, and a crash jarred me out of my reverie. The chapel shuddered.

"The oak," Mom said. "Lightning must have hit the old oak by the back door. I felt in my bones this morning that a rain was coming but I didn't know it was going to be a storm like this."

The tree seemed to have landed on the roof. I hoped it would not come through.

Mom squeezed my arm. "Darcy, I am sorry that you have had such a sad welcome home. I wanted you to feel safe here."

"I will admit that finding a dead body and being in the middle of the storm of the century is a little different than I imagined," I said. "It is, however, a homecoming I'll never forget."

Actually, it was more than memorable—horrible came to mind. And, "safe" was not a good description of the way I felt at the moment. Would a storm obliterate us or would Ben's murderer get to us first?

Was it only this morning that the neighbor's old gray mule had brayed a welcome to a beautiful spring day? The sun had dappled the leaves of the maple in Mom's front yard and brought out the heavenly scent of peonies by the gate. Standing beside those bushes more than twenty years ago, my boyfriend had kissed me for the first time. Not Jake; not at that time. It was tall, slim, and handsome Grant Hendley, the man of my girlhood dreams. Where was Grant now? Had life dealt well with him?

Mom interrupted my thoughts. "Listen, Darcy."

"I don't hear anything."

"Right. We don't hear anything. The storm is over!"

My knees wobbled when I stood up and my mother evidently felt the same. "I am as weak as a kitten," she said. "I guess that's what comes of being scared about half to death."

Taking her arm, I led her to the front door. "Let's see if your Toyota will start or if it has been washed down the hill and into the creek. I hope we can get back to town and there are no trees across the road."

"But, Darcy," Mom said, "you're forgetting poor Ben. Someone should stay with him. You go on home and get the sheriff. I'll stay."

I stared at her. "Are you kidding? I'm not letting you out of my sight. There is a murderer loose somewhere around here. Ben is dead and we can't help him now. My concern is for you. You need dry clothes and something hot to drink. We are both going into Levi and get the law out here as fast as we can."

Unlocking the door, I tugged it open. Grass swam with water. Rivulets ran here and there like small creeks. The huge oak lay at a crazy angle across the back of the roof, its roots sticking out of the mud. Faded flowers in forlorn little heaps were scattered among the graves and tangled in trees. Sunlight filtered through remnants of racing clouds. At the back of the cemetery, that mound of debris was still there but, thankfully, it was so far away that we could not distinguish Ben's body.

Mom sighed. "How in the world will we ever have things ready for Decoration Day? And how can we even have a Decoration when somebody has murdered poor Ben?"

I guided her around a water-filled hole. "It will be a job for your cemetery club. If anybody can set this place to rights again, it is you, Flora Tucker. Let's hurry. Who knows if the killer has gone or if he's somewhere around here."

She quickened her pace. I held the door as she slid into the passenger seat of her Toyota. Then I hurried to the driver's side, jumped in, and reached for the ignition. There was only one route back to Levi, and, hopefully, the little creek below the hill had not washed out the road.

CHAPTER 2

The return trip toward Levi was an adventure in itself. Water washed up on the car as we splashed across the creek, and the tires left deep ruts in red mud. I drove as fast as I dared, my need to contact law enforcement urging me onward. Finally, mud became a paved road and the Toyota picked up speed. Dodging a small tree across the asphalt, we snaked our way up Deertrack Hill. When we were at last on level ground, Mom tried the cell phone again. This time, it worked. She dialed the sheriff's office in Levi.

Even to me, her quavering recital about finding Ben sounded unbelievable, especially when she mentioned the missing finger. At last, she snapped the phone shut. "Grant said to stay right here and he will meet us. He wants us to go back to Goshen with him and Jim Clendon. That's Grant's deputy," she said.

"Grant?" I asked. "Grant who?"

"Why, Darcy, I thought you knew that Grant Hendley has been sheriff of Ventris County for a year now." She pointed to a small grocery store on the right side of the road. "Why not wait here in Tanner's parking lot for Grant?"

So, my old flame became the sheriff of his hometown. He would be good at the job. Always a staunch believer in right being right and wrong being wrong—that was Grant Hendley. Unaccountably, I thought about my hair, plastered down to my head by the rain. My shirt and jeans were still damp and mud clung to my shoes. Grant probably would not recognize me.

Driving onto the paved area, I shut off the ignition and slumped against the steering wheel. "I don't want to go back to the cemetery. Not today; not ever."

Mom patted my shoulder. "We are going to have to go back."

Closing my eyes, I asked, "Do you have an aspirin in your purse?"

The sun was playing hide and seek with harmless-looking clouds by the time the sheriff and his deputy arrived. Grant swung out of his truck and strode to our car, looking much the way I remembered him, only thinner. His eyes were as blue as ever, but gray sprinkled his red hair. Pushing his Stetson back from his forehead, he smiled, and an old, familiar warmth stirred in my heart—a disturbing feeling.

"Darcy," he said, "good to see you."

Returning his smile, I reached out to grasp his hand as he extended it through my window.

Jim Clendon squinted at me. "What's this about finding some poor devil dead on top of the ground at the cemetery? Don't you know that's unlawful? You're supposed to let 'em stay buried."

"Forgive me if I don't find that amusing," I said between clenched teeth. My head pounded like a kettledrum. Mom's aspirin had yet to work. "And," I added, "that is not 'some poor devil,' that's Ben Ventris lying out there."

Clendon grinned and shot a stream of tobacco juice into a puddle.

Mom threw me a warning glance. "I think we'd better just show you what we found, Grant."

Reluctantly, I put the car into gear and led the way back to our grim discovery. As we stopped once more at Goshen, only the thought of lending support to Mom gave me the courage to go through the gate.

Grant and his deputy parked beside us. "I see that the storm got the tool shed and that old oak," Clendon said.

"The tool shed can be replaced," Mom snapped. "What we can't replace is Ben lying dead out there." She pointed toward the tumble of branches that was Ben Ventris's coffin.

Halfway between the gate and the body, Mom and I stopped to watch Grant and Clendon wade through the grass toward that forlorn heap. They walked around, bending over the ground now and then, obviously searching for something. At one point, Clendon kicked a branch aside, then they both peered intently at the pile of debris where we found Ben.

At last, they came back to where we waited. What would be Grant's verdict? Would he find any clues?

An odd little smirk twitched the corner of Clendon's mouth. He pulled a wad of tobacco from the back pocket of his jeans, bit off a chew, and asked, "So, just where is this so-called body?"

Air whooshed from my lungs. "What do you mean?" I gasped.

Running through the sodden grass, I reached the place where Mom and I had uncovered Ben. My mother jogged along behind me. The jumble of branches, rocks, and dirt still covered the ground, but Ben was gone. Not even an indentation showed that a body had lain here.

Both men stared at Mom and me with strange expressions. Grant cleared his throat. "Miss Flora, Darcy, are you sure there was a body here? Nerves play tricks on us sometimes and even make us believe— well—storms make a person nervous and you just went through a bad one. Maybe you thought you saw something that wasn't really here."

Anger brought the blood to my face. Had Grant Hendley changed in those years since we were both teenagers? As I remembered, trust had been a large part of our relationship. How dare he insinuate we had made up a story about finding Ben?

Clendon wiped his mouth and snorted. "And, anyhow, are you for certain sure it was Ben Ventris, assuming that you did see somebody on that brush pile, which don't appear to be likely. If that there body was all covered up, how'd you come to recognize him?"

Grant shook his head. "Now, Jim, I've read some of Darcy's articles in the paper and she's a good investigative reporter. If she and Miss Flora think Ben Ventris was here, we'd better keep looking. Why don't you take a walk down the hill a way and see if you can find any sign of a body being moved or any drag marks or squashed vegetation. It's going to be hard to tell what the storm caused and what might have been made by something or somebody else." He turned toward us. "Are you pretty sure it was poor old Ventris?"

"There's no mistake about that, Grant," I said. "Mom has known Ben for a long time."

Clendon interrupted, giving my mother an up-and-down insinuating leer. "Yeah. I heard they were real good friends."

What did he mean by that? I was on the verge of stepping forward, grabbing Clendon's fox face, and twisting it around nineteen times.

Grant spoke sharply. "Jim, you go on down the hill and take a look. Now!"

Mom didn't seem to be aware of any insult. She continued staring at the pile of rubble, her breath raspy.

"Sit down over there, Mom," I ordered, indicating the flat top of a gravestone. Surely she wasn't going to faint. Her color was pasty.

She fanned her face with her hand, as if she found it hard to breathe. "This must be a nightmare, Darcy," she said. "It can't be real."

"Where did you get that deputy?" I asked Grant as Clendon sauntered down the hill. "Surely you had more candidates in the county that you could choose from."

"I apologize for Jim," Grant said. "Sometimes his choice of words isn't the best, but he's like a bulldog when it comes to going after the bad guys. Would you two ladies be willing to make a statement saying you saw Ventris under all this brush? Think about it before you answer. You say you found him, you say there was a bullet hole in his chest, and that he was missing a finger? Do you want to put your names to a statement like that?"

Stomping my foot sent water splashing from the rain-soaked grass. "Now listen to me, Grant Hendley. It's just like Mom and I told you. Ben isn't here now but he certainly was. A dead man named Ben Ventris was lying right out here in all these sticks and limbs before the storm hit. Why would we make up such a story? You know me better than that!"

Clendon sloshed back toward us. "Not a thing down the hill there, folks," he said. "If somebody dragged a body out of here, there sure isn't any sign of it now. Maybe the rain revived him and he just up and walked off."

I bit my tongue and glanced at Mom. She had begun to shiver and I started toward her, thinking that she had had enough for one day. As it turned out, indisputable proof of our story lay at my feet; proof that could provide positive identification of the body these two officers doubted had ever lain here.

I kicked some soggy leaves out of my way and froze in mid-stride. Although the grayish, swollen object floating in the mud puddle looked like nothing I had ever seen before—pulpy and misshapen— there was no doubt in my mind it could be only one thing—the finger of a human hand.

I beckoned to Grant then pointed at the ground. Nobody said a word. Even Clendon's sneer vanished. The only sound in the cemetery was a cardinal in a distant tree telling us to "Cheer up, Cheer up," and my mother, softly sobbing.

Finally, Grant broke the silence. "Okay. I reckon you were right. I'll take this to the lab boys and see what they tell me."

"Darcy," Mom whispered, "I want to go home."

We turned toward the gate.

"Hey! Hold on there!" yelled Clendon. "Where do you think you're going? We haven't gotten your written statement."

My cheeks burned and I spun on my heel. "You just hold on yourself," I said. "We are leaving. If you decide you want a written statement today, you know where my mother lives. If not, we'll see you tomorrow."

Mom and I walked away with as much dignity as two traumatized women could summon. I felt the gaze of both men boring into my back as we trudged toward Mom's car.

CHAPTER 3

Afternoon shadows pointed toward evening by the time I stopped the Toyota in Mom's driveway. Her old-fashioned two-story farmhouse had never looked so good. Every one of my mother's sixty-seven years showed on her face. The skin stretched tightly across her prominent cheekbones. For many years, her curly hair had been laced with white, but tonight those curls appeared limp and tired.

Climbing the porch steps, I unlocked the front door. "We both need warm baths and food," I said. "I'll scramble some eggs and make some coffee for supper."

She did not reply.

After showering, I slipped into blue jeans and a red long-sleeved sweatshirt and stepped into my favorite fuzzy blue house shoes. Being warm and dry made me feel nearly normal. The mirror above my dressing table showed a face that left no doubt as to my Cherokee ancestry. The older I got, the more I looked like my mother. I only hoped that at her age I had the stamina that kept her going. If would also be nice if I developed some of her faith.

Surprisingly, I looked a whole lot better than I felt. Two spots of color shone in my cheeks without the aid of a blusher. Somewhere, I had read that people who come into close contact with violent death and survive often feel and look unusually alive and vibrant. Of course, that psychology probably would not apply if the murder victim had been a lifelong friend.

Mom's old yellow coffee pot sat in its accustomed place on the counter in the kitchen. By the time she appeared, I was warming my hands around a steaming cup. I poured a mug full for her.

She looked doubtful. "I don't think I can drink this," she said.

"You need the caffeine," I assured her. "Something hot will make a new woman out of you."

Sinking into a chair, she said, "It's going to take a whole lot more than coffee to make me feel anything but old and bewildered."

I cracked two eggs into a bowl. "Let's have a bite to eat and then we'll talk. We need to be sure we're both clear on exactly what we saw and when we saw it, before we give our written statements tomorrow."

Mom's gaze slid toward the kitchen window but I had a feeling she wasn't seeing the apple tree in the yard. I needed to ask several questions and while I stirred the eggs, I pondered how to ask them without upsetting her further. "Had you seen Ben lately?" I asked.

She nodded.

"First, do you have any idea why someone would hate him enough to kill him and then do a gruesome thing like cutting off his finger?" I shuddered.

She closed her eyes for a second. "Probably his finger was cut off because somebody wanted the ring he wore and that was the only way they could get it. As far as his death, well, Ben had a premonition that might happen."

"Do you mean that somebody killed him in order to get a ring? That doesn't make any kind of sense, Mom."

"This wasn't just any ring, Darcy. It was, maybe, two hundred years old and worth more than a diamond the size of a possum grape."

The coffee I was about to swallow caught in my throat. Possum grapes grew wild along creek bottoms in Texas and Oklahoma, and although they weren't as large as Concords or wine grapes, they were bigger than a black-eyed pea. Grabbing hold of the idea of a gold ring worth more than a pea-sized diamond was hard.

"But, who would know that the ring would be worth that much?" I asked. "And what was so special about it?"

Mom passed her hand wearily over her forehead. "Very few people would know the value of that ring," she said. "That's why we need to look only at those few to find Ben's killer."

I opened my mouth to ask what she meant by "we" when it was clearly a job for the law; then, I thought better of it and let her go on with her story.

Mom stared at her mug, but her next words told me she was seeing far back into the past. "Ben's family has lived here in Oklahoma longer than most. They were here before the Cherokees arrived on the Trail of Tears. Ben's ancestors were part of the Old Settlers bunch. They came mostly to Arkansas in the early 1800s from the eastern states. Some of them settled in the territory before it became the state of Oklahoma. Ben's family came from Georgia, around the area where gold was mined."

"Gold? I never knew Georgia had gold."

"Neither did a lot of other people. According to old-timers, quite a bit of gold was taken out of the ground in Georgia beginning sometime in the 1500s, in a place called Nacoochee Valley."

My mother, the historian. "So, how did you come to learn all this and why didn't I know before now?"

She smiled. "Ben told me a lot, but, you forget, my dear daughter, that I've lived for a long time in these hills and you and I had Cherokee ancestors too. I liked to listen to stories my dad told. Anyway, at first, Ben's family kept the nuggets because they were beautiful, but when they found out that non- Indians would steal or kill to get their hands on them, they decided they'd better quit talking about the gold. Some of Ben's people were goldsmiths. The ring Ben wore came from his father and grandfather before him. All I know for sure is that the gold in that ring is from Georgia and was engraved with some sort of symbol."

Pausing, she swallowed more coffee. "Ben said a little silver mixed with the gold when it was being formed in the ground. There's no other gold like it anywhere and that's what the ring was made of. It came from the area around Dahlonega, Georgia. Dahlonega means 'yellow' or 'place of the yellow' in the Cherokee language. It's very valuable."

Mom spoke so softly I had to strain to hear her. What an amazing story, and to think that I had never heard it before!

Scooting her chair away from the table, she went to a cabinet over the refrigerator and pulled out a small red and black tin box, her old recipe box. She returned to her chair and drew a wrinkled leather drawstring bag from among the recipes. She turned the bag upside-down and a gold ring rolled onto the table.

"This ring is a little different than Ben's," she said. "It's made from the same kind of gold and is about as old as Ben's ring. See this scrollwork? It is supposed to bring me peace and happiness."

Picking up the small circlet, I held it under the light and studied it. A greenish-yellow glow shone with subdued brilliance. With a million questions in my mind and on the tip of my tongue, I turned to my mother but she answered before I could ask.

"Yes, Ben gave me that ring many years ago, for my seventeenth birthday. He wanted me to keep it as a symbol of our friendship. Although I don't believe happiness comes from a ring, no matter how valuable, I kept it because it was from Ben. He clung to the old ways, the Cherokee ways."

Swallowing a couple of times, at last I said, "But a ring! Doesn't that mean some sort of commitment? I mean, even fifty years ago . . . ."

Mom's eyes twinkled. "Darcy, did you ever stop to think that maybe you don't know everything about this family? Way back then, before I ever met your father, Ben and I were sweethearts."

If she had said the donkey across the road who insisted on braying his head off was a dinosaur, I could not have been more shocked. Surely, my mother had never loved anybody else but my father, Andy Tucker. Their marriage had seemed perfect to me, two people who were destined for each other. Never would I have imagined she had any other suitor. Yet, here she was, confessing that she had!

"Even after we married other people, Ben's family and Andy and I remained friends. Your father said he had never known a finer man than Ben Ventris."

Shaking my head, I hurried to turn off the heat under the scorched eggs. I would have to start again on our supper.

Mom traced the rim of her mug with her finger, speaking as if she were talking to herself. "I saw Ben fairly often these last few years. He and I knew the same people and we were both lonely, but that's all we were, just good friends. Sometimes, we went for drives along the river; sometimes, we just sat on the porch and talked. But now, that is all over and it's mighty hard to accept."

For the life of me, I could not think of an adequate response.

Once more gazing out of the window, she continued, "It must have been a couple of weeks ago that Ben stopped in and we talked about gold. He told me that I should keep quiet about what he was telling me, that nobody must ever find out that he had let me in on the secret or I might be in danger too, as he felt he was. He said he had some items made from Dahlonega gold and that they were worth a lot of money. Ben believed in "warnings" as he called them. He said he had a feeling that bad things were going to happen to him and he wanted to be sure somebody knew about the treasure he had and where it was. He didn't trust lawyers. He told his daughter, Skye, about the gold's hiding place. She was the only one who knew, besides Ben himself."

My head was swimming. I gingerly touched the gold ring on the table. "Are you saying there are more gold items besides Ben's ring and this one?"

Mom shrugged. "I don't have any idea how many relics are left, but Ben did say there's a bunch and they are worth a lot of money."

"Did he give you any idea of where that stuff is?"

"No. He said he would ask Skye to mail a map to me. He trusted me and he wanted me not to even look at the map unless something bad happened to both him and his daughter. Skye lives in Oklahoma City."

I interrupted. "Ben never lived like a rich man."

"Ben was just Ben," Mom said, smiling. "He preferred the old ways. He wouldn't have been comfortable any other way. However, he was able to send Skye to the University of Oklahoma, and I never knew her to want for anything in her whole life."

The setting sun warmed Mom's west kitchen window and painted the sky in varying shades of chartreuse, purple, and crimson. That same lovely sunset would be lighting Goshen Cemetery too. My mind strayed to the storm-damaged grounds and building and that strangely empty jumble of tree branches and brush. What had happened to Ben's body? Somebody must have taken him away but why? And how? And where? Most of all, who?

Mom broke the silence. "Ben said the knowledge of the gold's hiding place was passed down from generation to generation; in fact, to only one person in each generation. I feel honored that he broke that tradition by including me in knowing about the hiding place."

"I don't agree, Mom! I think it was selfish of Ben. If he was killed for more than that gold ring, your knowing the secret of the hiding place may have put you in danger. Maybe somebody was trying to make him tell where the rest of it is hidden. Or maybe they succeeded in finding out and killed him anyway. Thank goodness he didn't tell you. If you knew, and if Ben was actually killed because he wouldn't divulge the location of that gold, your life could be in danger!" I got up and started pacing the floor. What had Ben Ventris been thinking? How dare he even mention that gold to my mother? Why couldn't he have just kept quiet?

Slowly, my mother shook her head. "Now, Darcy, don't get all upset. Nobody except Skye would know that Ben talked to me about the gold. Besides, that's beside the point now. I don't give a hoot about any old treasure. I want to know who killed Ben!"

"Sure, Mom, so do I, but I still can't help wishing . . . ."

"Ben was a lot deeper than he seemed," Mom said. "He even owned some oil lands in western Oklahoma at one time. Maybe he used part of the gold to buy them; I don't know, but he didn't want the responsibility of being rich. He gave all that oil land to his daughter."

I stopped pacing and leaned against the table. "I wonder if the killer tortured the hiding place out of Ben before he shot him."

"I don't think so, Darcy. Ben would never have told. But killing Ben would be like killing the goose that laid the golden egg, seems to me."

"Murder is always an insane act," I said. "What if Ben's killer has a terrible temper? What if he became so angry at Ben for not telling, that he just shot him?"

"And lose hope of ever finding the gold? It doesn't make sense to me."

I took my cold coffee to the sink and dumped it before refilling my cup. "No, it doesn't make sense, none of it does. Let's go to bed and try to forget this terrible day, at least for a few hours."

My mother showed no inclination to follow my suggestion. "Ben was superstitious. He believed in Jesus, but those old ways of his ancestors were hard to sluff off. He mentioned something about an owl and an omen. He kept feeling that someone was watching him. Maybe there were other reasons he was afraid, but that's what he told me."

"I guess old beliefs are hard to shake, even if they don't make sense in today's world," I said. "Owls are my favorite bird and certainly would not be an omen. I like to hear them."

"I do too," Mom said. "To me, they are just another of God's wonderful creations."

"If you feel like staying up for a few more minutes, I'd like to jot down your answers to some questions, Mom."

She nodded.

Finding a notebook and pencil in the catch-all drawer under her cabinet, I again sat down at the table, feeling much as I did when covering a story for *The Dallas Morning News*."

"Okay, Mom. Ben told you he had a fortune in gold relics hidden somewhere?" I asked, scribbling in the notebook. "He said he suspected something was going to happen to him? Didn't he ever give you a hint where the treasure might be or who would want to know and be willing to commit murder for the information?"

"Not a clue," Mom said. "He told me it was dangerous to know and I would have that information when I heard from Skye, but I was not to tell a single soul about it."

If Ben hadn't been dead, I think I would have given him a piece of my mind. If he cared for my mother, why on earth would he risk putting her in danger?

"Do you think it would be hidden somewhere near his house?" I asked.

"Could be," she said. "His farm is awash in springs and caves and creeks and, of course, there's the river. There are hiding places all over Ben's land. I wouldn't know where to begin to look."

I put down my pencil. "We don't have any guarantee it is on Ben's land. Maybe it's somewhere else. Do you know for sure that the gold or whatever is in Ventris County?"

"It makes sense that it would be, Darcy. This is the area where many of our Cherokee ancestors settled. Personally, I don't care where it is or who finds it. I just want that evil person who killed Ben Ventris brought to justice." She rubbed her head and yawned. "All of a sudden, I'm so tired, I don't think I can keep my eyes open."

Sending her to bed, I cleaned up the kitchen. We hadn't eaten supper but probably neither of us could have managed food. When at last I crawled between my sheets, I realized how exhausted I was. It seemed I'd been awake for three days, but even though I was worn out, I couldn't sleep. During the night, I heard Mom prowling around and knew she wasn't resting either.

Raising my window, I heard tree frogs singing their nightly praise to spring. Somewhere deep in a shadowed hollow, a whippoorwill called and, in the distance, another answered. As I listened, the soft questioning voice of an owl drifted in with the breeze. Wasn't it Shakespeare who said, "Sleep knits up the raveled sleeve of care?" Well, my sleeve of care felt shredded, but when sleep finally got out her knitting needles, it seemed only a few minutes before the neighbor's punctual gray mule brayed me awake. He was louder than any rooster or alarm clock.

Swinging my feet to the floor, I got up and tiptoed past Mom's door. Her gentle snore told me that at last sleep had overtaken her. Downstairs, I cranked up my computer. A Google search showed a lot of hits for Dahlonega gold. The articles I found confirmed what Mom had told me. The greenish-yellow gold was rare and pricey. Was it so valuable that someone would kill for it? I knew the answer to that. People committed murder for far less. I wanted no part of it. Mom didn't either, but she seemed determined to find the identity of Ben's killer. This was a dangerous determination and I hoped I could talk her out of it.

CHAPTER 4

A week after Ben's death, our lives had returned to as nearly normal as possible. The murder of Mom's dear friend hung like a dark cloud over us. Grant and his deputies were no closer to finding the killer than they had been when we made the discovery of Ben's body. Bad news travels fast and our part in this mystery spread quickly throughout the county. Mom's phone rang with a lot of curious people wanting to know the particulars, details that had not made the papers.

Finally, I told each caller that the sheriff had sworn us to secrecy and suggested they call his office. His secretary would not love me for that but I was desperate. Decoration Day, the third Sunday in May, was just around the corner and we had to turn our minds to that. Mom had contacted other members of the board who took care of maintenance at Goshen. She was determined that, come Decoration Sunday, the grounds would be as neat as they could be, the tree and tool shed would be hauled away, and the roof at least temporarily repaired.

Sitting down in front of my computer in the living room, I tried to type a rough draft of the article I had agreed to write for *The Dallas Morning News*. I called it "The Changing Face of Rural America." Since my roots sank deep into this small town in Oklahoma which retained more of its twentieth-century culture than most, my editor figured I was the perfect person to write about the impact of modern technology on the lives of country folk. Writing the article was a welcome diversion from grief over Jake and being concerned that a killer roamed Ventris County.

A movement out of the large picture window caught my eye. A dark blue Buick rolled slowly down Graham Road. Not a lot of people came this way unless Mom's house was their destination. Our road dead-ended at the Barker place about a mile past us. Maybe the driver was from out of town and was lost.

Pausing at Mom's mailbox, the car then pulled into her circular driveway. A man got out and peered at the house. He was tall and broad, and he wore charcoal pants and a pale gray jacket. He moved like a *yonah*, a bear. Instead of putting his weight first on his heel as he strode toward the house, he walked flat-footed, slapping each foot down in a manner that spoke of arrogance. Few strangers approached my mother's door, and this fellow gave me a prickle of apprehension. Since the murder, we were suspicious of anyone we did not know.

"Mom!" I called toward the kitchen. "We have a visitor. Were you expecting somebody?"

When the bell rang, I opened the wood door, being sure the storm door was locked. My mother came right along behind me.

"Mrs. Campbell and Mrs. Tucker?" the man asked in a low, guttural voice. Without waiting for our answer, he said, "I'm special agent Ray Drake of the Federal Bureau of Investigation."

"Do you have any identification?" I asked.

Mom whispered, "Darcy, he said he's from the FBI for goodness sake."

I frowned at her. This person was not coming in just yet. My mother was entirely too trusting.

He held up a card and a badge which looked authentic, but many things could be replicated on today's computers. Information on the card confirmed that he was from the FBI's Southwest Regional District. Guessing that he was based in Dallas, I determined to use my newspaper connections to check him out if he proved to be less than open with us. I glanced at the bookshelf where my father's old handgun lay hidden in a drawer.

Drake managed a tight smile. "I don't blame you for being cautious. I won't take much of your time. I want to ask you some questions about the murder of Ben Ventris."

Now my curiosity was piqued. "There's not much to tell, Mr. Drake. My mother and I just happened to be at the cemetery and . . . ."

Mom pushed around me and held open the door. "Oh, for Pete's sake, Darcy. Come on in, Mr. Drake. I want to know why the FBI is interested in Ben Ventris."

I backed against the bookshelf as his bulk filled the doorway.

"Thanks, Ma'am," Drake growled.

"I've just made a pot of coffee. Sit down right there on the sofa and I'll bring you a cup," said my mother, smiling broadly.

What was wrong with her? This man was a stranger and we had only his word and a small card to back up the claim that he was who he said. Hospitality was Mom's byword, but she was going overboard. I remembered the smile she wore from days gone by when I was a teenager and she pumped me about my social life. Two of her wise sayings I had heard since childhood popped into my memory: "You catch more flies with honey than with vinegar," and "Full stomach; loose tongue." Next, she would probably bring him a slice of her pound cake. And that is exactly what she did.

I think she shocked our visitor, but he recovered nicely. Drake mumbled, "Thanks." The grimace that crossed his face must have been his version of a smile.

Folding my arms across my chest, I leaned against the bookshelf. "Mr. Drake, I don't understand why you are coming to us. We told the sheriff everything we know. I suggest you contact him. And, by the way, how did you know about our involvement in the case and how to find us?"

Drake swallowed a large chunk of cake. "I plan to visit with Sheriff Hendley, and all I had to do was read the local newspaper to find out how you two figured in this investigation. When I asked for directions, everyone was willing to tell me where you live."

"If you have read the newspaper articles, you know as much about Ben Ventris's death as we do. It is all a sad mystery and we were unlucky enough to discover his body," I said.

Drake swallowed the last crumb of cake and drained his coffee. His question was directed toward my mother. "So, you knew the dead man very well, Mrs. Tucker?"

Mom sniffed. "Let's call him by his name. Yes, Ben and I had been friends for many years."

"And had you seen him recently?" he asked.

Mom squirmed on her chair and pleated the hem of her shirt with her fingers. "Let me see now . . . he was at the church Christmas party back in December but I don't think . . . you know, he didn't get out a whole lot after his wife died. Most times he'd just come to town on Friday afternoons and get a few groceries, maybe some dog food for that big hound of his. According to Harry Blanchard down at the Shell station, he didn't even stop to drink coffee any more like he used to do. He just pretty much kept to himself and liked it that way."

Her voice trailed off. I stared at her. My mother, who rated Truth at the top of her scale of virtues, was lying. I knew it and so must Agent Drake, but that meant she did not really trust this FBI agent either.

"Ben spoke of having an FBI relative somewhere. Are you related to Ben? Seems I see a resemblance around the nose," she said, tilting her chin and surveying his face.

Agent Drake's dark eyebrows drew down. "Mrs. Tucker, I don't believe . . . ."

I interrupted. "I'm having a little trouble figuring out something here."

His head swiveled in my direction. "And that would be?"

"Ben Ventris was a poor, lonely man without much family."

Our visitor didn't need to know that Ben may have been lonely but he certainly wasn't poor.

"It's very disturbing that he was murdered but it sounds to me like a case for local authorities, or maybe even the state police, but why your agency? The FBI has jurisdiction in cases where federal law is broken or contraband or weapons are transported across state lines or there is a theft that involves federally insured money, that sort of thing. So, Mr. Drake, can you tell us more about your interest in this matter?"

He crossed his legs and leaned against the back of the sofa. A dull red crept up his neck as he looked down his nose at me.

"I am sure, Mrs. Campbell, that you realize I am not at liberty to discuss an ongoing investigation."

"I do understand," I said, making a point of gazing directly into his squinty eyes. "I also know that the law requires an investigating officer to reveal to the subject under interrogation the basic reasons why said officer needs the information he is requesting."

If eyes could smolder, his did. Anger burned in them. "Your mother is not being interrogated and neither are you. I'm trying to get a little background here, Mrs. Campbell. I understand that you were a reporter and you should know that we must explore all possibilities. Now, may I continue?"

I nodded. He would get his information from us or from someone else. Maybe it was better if we had control of the answers.

Drake turned toward Mom and began again in a matter-of-fact voice. "According to my sources, Ventris was here at your house Mrs. Tucker, on the evening of Thursday, May 4. Is that correct?"

My mother's eyes widened. "That's not . . . ."

Drake's voice was low and probing, like a dentist asking if he was pecking on a sore tooth. "Not what, Mrs. Tucker? Not the story you just told me?"

My mother's mouth scrunched up as if she had tasted quinine. An alarm bell went off in my mind. How had this man known about Ben's last visit? That fact had not appeared in the paper. Mom had told no one but Grant Hendley and me; yet Drake said he had not talked to Grant; besides, Grant would never divulge such information.

"And just why do you think that?" I cracked open the bookshelf drawer behind me.

Drake actually smirked. "We have ways of finding out even the smallest things, Mrs. Campbell. You see, we know that Ventris and your mother were close friends and friends sometimes share confidences. Nobody seems to know why Ventris was killed. I wonder if Mrs. Tucker would have any inkling why somebody would hurt a harmless fellow like Ben Ventris? I wonder if he told her anything that's weighing on her mind, anything that might have been dangerous to the poor deceased. I've a feeling your mother knows more than she's saying, Mrs. Campbell."

The drawer pull bit into my back as I eased it out enough to get my hand inside. My fingers closed around the cold metal of Dad's pistol. This man, this Ray Drake, thought my mother knew something that had caused Ben's death. Did he know about the cache of gold? His professionalism had slipped. I did not know his purpose, but I did not doubt he wasn't who he said he was.

Drake was not finished with his questions. "Did you know, Mrs. Tucker that Ventris went to New York City just last month and stayed for two days?"

I gulped. Never would I have guessed that Ben had been out of the state, much less to a far-off place like New York. Mom, however, did not bat an eyelash.

"Of course," she said. "Since you know so much about Ben and about me too, seems like, you surely know that I fed Ben's dog while he was gone."

Deceptively gentle, Drake probed on. "Since you were the best of friends, and you knew he made the trip to New York City, I'm sure you know why he went."

Mom shook her head.

He frowned and leaned toward my mother, "Come on, now, Mrs. Tucker. Surely he told you."

Speaking with a calmness I did not feel, I said, "Mr. Drake, my mother and I have appointments. I am going to ask you to leave. Now."

Drake's face turned purple but he got to his feet and started for the door. Turning, he glared at me and made a valiant effort to reclaim his coolness. He put a business card on the bookshelf beside me.

"This has my telephone number on it," he said. "If you think of anything you feel would be helpful, give me a call. Sometimes secrets eat away at a person and can even be dangerous to your health."

Was he threatening us? I locked the door behind him, sure of two things: Ray Drake was not from the FBI and he believed that Mom had some vital information that he wanted. What was that information? The location of the hidden gold? It looked to me as if my mother's friendship with Ben Ventris had turned into a dangerous thing.

CHAPTER 5

"Darcy, were you going to point your dad's gun at Ray Drake?" Mom asked.

I turned from watching that big blue Buick disappear down the street. "Only if I felt we were in immediate danger, Mom."

She frowned. "Where is your faith in God's protection?"

Where indeed? Had I even prayed when I became suspicious of Drake?

"I should have more faith," I admitted. "It was just a gut reaction to that man's hatefulness. I guess I didn't think of prayer. Why didn't you tell me about Ben's trip to New York?"

She shrugged. "I just forgot about it. The trip was last month. I don't think it could have anything to do with Ben's death, do you?"

"I don't know. I don't think Ray Drake is with the FBI but he is certainly after what we know about Ben. He must have heard about that gold, but how?"

"The story of lost gold has been circulating around town for decades. Oldtimers may have put it down to being a fable and I doubt that many remember it at all," Mom said. "Ben told me the secret of the hiding place was passed down from generation to generation to only one member of his family. Nobody outside the family would take it seriously. They'd think it was an interesting tale but nothing to get excited about. He didn't tell me his reason for his trip. He said he'd tell me later, but he never did."

"Are you sure that Ben's daughter is the last of Ben's family? Could there be anybody else, some far-flung relative who might have remembered that Ben had hidden wealth? He didn't really tell you he had an FBI relative, did he?"

She raised her eyebrows and looked at the ceiling. "No, he didn't, may the Lord forgive me. Ben's parents, his wife, his brother, they are all dead. There was a nephew, but he left Oklahoma years ago." She shook her head. "Elijah Ventris. Folks called him Hammer. I hadn't thought about him in years."

"Do you think Skye would know why her dad went to New York?"

"Maybe," Mom said. "Ben gave me her phone number. It's around here somewhere. We could call and ask if she knows."

She left the room and a few minutes later, came back with a small, embossed card. Taking it from her hand, I read that Skye Ventris was a psychiatrist in a top-rated hospital in Oklahoma City. Maybe she would have a free moment and could talk to me. It was worth a try.

Dialing the number, I waited until a receptionist answered, informing me that I had reached the office of Dr. Skye Ventris and yes, she would see if the doctor was available.

Skye, I remembered, was a few years older than I. In high school, I was in awe of this beautiful teenager, a cheerleader at the time, with olive skin and long, silky black hair. She had come to Levi as soon as Grant told her of Ben's death, but I had not seen her then.

Her voice was warm. "Of course, I remember you, Darcy."

When I asked if she knew the reason for Ben's trip to New York, she seemed eager to talk.

"I have been so upset about Dad that I haven't realized the possible implications of that trip. In fact, he didn't tell me what he learned while he was there. Dad had a family heirloom that he was particularly curious about and he wanted an expert's opinion. I must come to Levi soon and have a long chat with Miss Flora. Dad gave me a map that he wanted her to have in case something happened to him. I'm afraid the map isn't worth much except as a curiosity. There's another document that is far more important. So, if I can't get away from my practice in a day or two, I'll drop them in the mail."

Her voice quavered. "My work is all that is saving my sanity. When I'm not busy, the whole horrible thing keeps replaying itself in my mind."

Skye talked for ten minutes and, after she hung up, I turned to Mom who was fidgeting on the sofa beside me. "Well?" she asked. "What did Skye say?"

"Ben had gone to see an antiquities dealer, an Arlen Templeton of Forrestal Antiquities, to get an estimate on the value of a certain family heirloom. Skye gave me that address, in New York City. She had not talked to Ben about what he found out. I'm going to see if I can get an airline ticket on short notice. I'm going to the Big Apple."

Biting her lip, Mom shook her head. "Do you think it's necessary?"

"You want to find Ben's killer, don't you?"

She nodded.

"Then we can't leave any stone unturned. I'll be fine. Remember, flying is safer than driving."

Sighing, she said, "But car wrecks don't happen 30,000 feet in the air."

I ruffled her curls and went to pull the telephone book out of its drawer. Tulsa might be the nearest airport, or maybe Highfill, Arkansas.

"At least, take Grant with you," Mom said.

"No, thanks. I don't want to spend a lot of time alone with Grant. Something tells me he would need very little encouragement to take up where we left off, and I'm not ready for that."

She was actually wringing her hands as I made my reservation. I would fly out of Arkansas.

"Darcy, I could go with you. If the plane went down with you on it, I'd want to be on it too."

Hugging her, I said, "I appreciate that, Mom, but you would be petrified and I don't think the plane is going to go down. However, it's not a good idea to leave you alone for two days. Please pack a bag and go to Aunt Bet's. In fact, I can drop you off there before I catch the plane."

Aunt Bet was no relation, but she and Mom had been friends for years. She lived in Fayetteville and it would work well for my mother to stay with her while I was out of town.

For a wonder, Mom needed no persuasion.

At two o'clock the next afternoon, after a much smoother flight than I expected, and after a Pakistani driver who seemed to think he was taking part in the Indianapolis 500 delivered me to the wide front door of Forrestal Antiquities Group, 621 East Kimball Circle, I stepped out of the cab and felt much like an ant among giant redwood trees. Skyscrapers towered above me and the roar of traffic and the din of honking horns beat on my eardrums.

Entering the lobby, I consulted a brass-plated directory near the security desk. I had phoned a newspaper colleague in this big city before I came. From him, I learned that New York was the antiquities group's main headquarters for its worldwide operation. It was no surprise, then, to find that Forrestal occupied the entire eleventh floor. Separate suites were indicated for Human Resources, Financial, and Benefits. The other side of that floor was allocated to Appraisals, Purchasing, and Consulting.

With the elevators as my destination, I said a silent prayer that Mr. Arlen Templeton could throw some light on a mystery that seemed to grow more complex with every piece of information we dug up. Reaching the eleventh floor, I stepped off the elevator into a lobby tastefully decorated in what could be described as subdued opulence. A velvety gray carpet muffled my steps as I approached the front desk. The receptionist was underwhelmed with the press card I presented. Technically, I still worked for *The Morning News,* just not on a full-time basis.

"I need information about a gold heirloom," I told her, "and Arlen Templeton is the only person who can give me that information."

The receptionist glanced from my card to me. "Mr. Templeton is in a meeting," she said, her voice sounding bored. "I'll find out whether Mr. Fredricks can see you."

Evidently, I needed to project a different demeanor, a warmer, friendlier, woman-to-woman approach. Leaning across her desk, I lowered my voice. "I just love your hair. So sophisticated." I hoped the Lord would forgive me; this was for a good cause.

The receptionist's nameplate read, "Minda Stilley."

"Ms. Stilley," I said, "it's so hard to get a decent haircut, isn't it? But I imagine you know lots of the best places here in New York. Could you recommend somebody?"

Her long, lime green iridescent fingertips caressed her black-as-shoe-polish hair. "Well," she said, "I usually go to Antonio's on Riverside Drive."

She stared at my version of a French twist. "I can see that your hair is thick and naturally wavy and inclined to frizz."

Boy! Was she right about that!

"You probably just need a good styling," she decided as she wrote on the back of the card I had handed her. She scribbled the address of Antonio's and returned it to me.

"Thanks," I said. "Listen, I actually need to see Mr. Templeton about a case that involves a murder that happened a few days ago."

Minda Stilley's eyes widened.

"I'm sure gals in your position know everything about the ins and outs of this business and can bend a few rules. Could you figure out some way I could talk to Mr. Templeton this afternoon? It's really important. My problem involves a man from out of state who met with Mr. Templeton the last part of April. Shortly afterward, he was murdered. Since the man was possibly one of your clients, you can understand that it's necessary that I speak to Mr. Templeton about Mr. Ventris."

Her lips formed a perfect O. "You—do you mean Mr. *Ben* Ventris?"

Bingo! Somebody within the company had evidently been notified of Ben's death. It was significant that the death of an unassuming man from northeast Oklahoma had been noted in this metropolitan empire.

When I nodded, Ms. Stilley lifted the telephone receiver. "I'll see what I can work out." She spoke softly into the mouthpiece and turned back to me.

"Mr. Templeton can spare you a few minutes, Ms. Campbell."

I gave her my biggest smile. "Just call me Darcy. And thanks so much for your help—for all your help." I patted my flyaway hair.

Minda Stilley grinned and gestured toward the hallway. "The fourth door on your right."

Arlen Templeton was waiting for me. He was a tall, slender man with thin, sandy hair and sharp blue eyes that would not miss many gnats on the wall. He wasted no time with preliminaries.

Stretching out his hand, he said, "Mrs. Campbell, good to meet you. You want to talk about Ben Ventris?"

He waved me toward a burgundy leather chair. "I was shocked to learn of Mr. Ventris's passing. Murdered? Unbelievable."

Guessing that this straight-talking man would appreciate nothing less than the truth from me, I dropped my bag on the floor, looked him in the eye, and began.

"Mr. Templeton, let me be honest. I do work for *The Dallas Morning News* as my press card says, but only on a freelance basis. I'm not here in any professional capacity. I'm here because I am very worried. Ben Ventris was a close friend of my mother's."

I proceeded to tell him all the gruesome details of Ben's death and included my fear that Mom's life might now be in danger.

"Why did Mr. Ventris come to see you, Mr. Templeton? The man is dead and his reason for coming all the way to New York may have some bearing on tracing down his murderer."

Arlen Templeton stared at me for a few seconds. "I will certainly help all I can, although I would think that your local police should be delving into his murder, not you, young lady."

An astute observation. "I don't think our authorities know that Ben came to see you. Until I find out whether his visit was important in finding his killer, I'd just as soon the Ventris County sheriff didn't know."

I trusted Grant but couldn't say the same for Jim Clendon. Who knew how he would react to whatever news Arlen Templeton was about to give me?

Arlen Templeton's eyes narrowed. "Isn't this unlawful, hiding facts that may be pertinent to a felony?"

Evasion seemed to be the best response. "I don't know what the facts are yet." As far as I knew, Grant had never heard any legends about Ben being the keeper of a treasure.

Gazing at me for a few more seconds, Mr. Templeton seemed to be mulling over what and how much he should tell me. At last, he pulled a manila folder from the top drawer of his desk and opened it.

"Mr. Ventris brought an unusual artifact to show me and he wanted to know its worth," he said. "That particular item was outside my area of expertise and I had to refer him to somebody else."

I scooted to the edge of my chair. "What was the artifact?"

"It was a medallion; perhaps a ceremonial item." Mr. Templeton lifted a page from his folder and slid it across the desk. "I made a photo of it because it was so unusual."

Made with a high-quality digital camera, the picture was clear, showing minute details. For size comparison, the artifact lay beside a man's hand. It was perhaps an inch and a half wide, and probably five inches long. An etching in the center of the medallion appeared to be a snake with strange designs around it. A loop was melded into the top of the medallion, presumably so that it could be worn around someone's neck. The color was a deep gold with a hint of green, leaving no doubt in my mind that the gold was the same as that in my mother's ring.

Glancing from the photo to Mr. Templeton, I said, "This gold is an odd color."

He nodded. "And with good reason. It has that distinctive cast because it's very likely mixed with a small amount of pure silver. I'm sure you know that gold in its natural state is too soft to be made into jewelry or anything else."

"It has to be mixed with a dab of steel or something," I offered, trying not to show my ignorance of the subject.

Mr. Templeton nodded. "Exactly. But the metals commonly used to give gold strength are always metallic colored so it doesn't really alter the color of the gold. You may have noticed that some gold is a pale yellow but the hue always depends on the mix. This gold, however, must have been melded naturally with silver because the medallion is ancient; so old, in fact, that it seems impossible it was blended by today's methods."

"So, could it be that the gold was mixed with a little pure silver while it was forming in the ground?" I asked.

He nodded. "Yes, that's what I told Mr. Ventris I suspected. Our firm hasn't had enough experience with it to be more than just speculative."

Templeton's office was a haven of stillness in the noisy rush of traffic in this metropolis. And, for a moment, I was aware only of the tick-tock of the grandfather clock sitting in a corner.

Templeton tented his fingers together. "The gold with the small amount of silver occurs naturally in only one part of the country that I'm aware of. It is a near a small town in Georgia called Dahlonega."

This fit exactly with what Mom had told me and what I had unearthed in my Google search. My head was swimming. "So, items made from this particular gold are worth a lot of money."

Templeton laughed. "Any kind of gold is worth a lot of money but this—yes, it is pretty pricey stuff."

Mom said that Ben had told her there were more gold items besides the two rings. I knew now that at least one gold medallion could be added to the stash.

"Since these items are so rare," Templeton continued, "most firms really don't have enough in-depth knowledge to deal with them. I had to refer Mr. Ventris to an expert who is actually nearer his home. In fact, if I had known what he had to show me when he called for an appointment, I could have saved him the trip to New York. The name I gave him was Jason Allred, a man in Oklahoma City who specializes in southern and southwestern antiquities. I can give you his office address if you'd like."

He scribbled on a small notepad, tore off a sheet, and handed it to me.

"Do you have any idea where Mr. Ventris got that medallion?" I asked.

"No," he said, shaking his head, "and I was too smart to ask. I doubt that anybody else knows either. Ben Ventris appeared to be a pretty shrewd man who told others only what was necessary." He paused. "Well, that's not exactly true. He did say that he had a trunk full of other such items."

Choking, I whispered, "A trunk full? What kind of trunk? There are trunks and then, there are *trunks*."

Mr. Templeton glanced at his watch. "I have no idea how many gold pieces he was talking about, but I'm guessing he meant more than a few."

I stood up. "Only one more question, Mr. Templeton. You've told me plainly that you're not an expert in the field of artifacts such as this." I pointed toward the photograph. "But if you were to make an educated guess, what kind of monetary figure would you attach to that?"

Templeton rose too. He gazed at me intently as he spoke. "If the origin of this gold can be determined—and that shouldn't be hard since all gold carries abnormalities peculiar to the location where it was mined—if Mr. Allred can document it and the provenance can be proven, then I'm guessing . . . ." He stared out of his window at two pigeons preening their feathers on the window ledge, then he tapped the photograph on his desk. "I'm guessing this little item is worth somewhere in the neighborhood of a million dollars."

Collapsing into the chair I had just vacated, air whooshed from my lungs. When I could speak, I said, "So, anybody who owned a trunk *full* of these items would be . . . ." Words failed me.

Mr. Templeton smiled and offered his hand to help me to my feet. "Quite wealthy? Yes, my dear Mrs. Campbell, it quite takes one's breath away, doesn't it?"

CHAPTER 6

The flight from New York to Arkansas passed quickly as I mulled over what I had learned. What was I to do with this information about Ben and the gold? As far as I was concerned, the gold should remain in its secret lair. The only one who knew its hiding place was Ben's daughter and I wanted to keep it that way. Skye evidently didn't need it; she had her dad's oil land and her own private practice. Something about the history of the gold seemed almost sacred and I didn't feel that it should be disturbed. Somehow, that gold was entwined with Ben's murder. My only interest was that Ben's killer be caught, quickly, before he murdered anyone else in his pursuit of riches.

Mom was waiting for me at Aunt Bet's in Fayetteville and as we drove back to Levi, I filled her in on what Arlen Templeton told me.

For a time, she was silent as trees and streams rushed past the Passport's windows. "There's someone in Oklahoma City who knows about the medallion?" she asked.

"Yes," I answered, "a Jason Allred."

Her mouth set in a determined line. "Then we must go see Mr. Allred."

"No, that might not be a good idea. The more we know about the gold, the more dangerous it becomes for you. Already, Ray Drake thinks you know more than you do."

Glancing at Mom's expression, I had the sinking feeling that soon we would be making the trek to our state's capital. At the moment, the only trip I wanted to take was to the bathtub for a long soak. Why had I become involved in such intrigue?

My first thought, the next morning when I awoke, was that I must tell Jake about my trip to New York, then, with a sharp pain through my heart, I realized anew that I would never talk to Jake again.

Tears blurred the scene from my bedroom window. Mom's front yard was awash with the colors of peonies, azaleas, and lilacs. How could nature keep to its eternal cycle while my heart was breaking? Again, I asked the Lord why He had taken Jake from me. How could I trust a God Who would do such a cruel thing? The morning offered no answers, so I wiped my eyes and slipped into my old blue robe. Tempting aromas of breakfast drifted up the stairs.

Mom sensed my mood. "Try these blueberry muffins," she said. "I'll pour your orange juice and coffee. Things will look better after you've eaten."

I sank down into a dining chair. "I don't know, Mom. Sometimes life itself is a mystery. How should we deal with all the bad things that happen?"

"Trust God, Darcy. He knows the end from the beginning. He knows all about Jake and He knows who killed Ben. That person will not escape the Lord's justice."

Biting into a muffin, I mumbled, "Maybe I'll drive out to Granny Grace's place today. It's always so peaceful out there."

"That's a good idea," she said. "You need some thinking time, and while you're doing that, I'll check in with the church thrift shop. They may want me to work today."

After washing the breakfast dishes, I went back upstairs, pulled on my blue jeans, a green knit shirt, and my hiking boots. Sometimes snakes hid in those rocks along the Ventris River, and I didn't intend to be bitten by one as I walked through the land that once belonged to my grandparents.

The phone rang just as I started out the front door. Grant's deep voice came across the wire.

"Is everything all right out your way, Darcy?"

How ridiculous and fickle of me that, even after intervening years, hearing Grant still brought back memories of soft spring nights and young dreams. Dangerous thoughts, those, and I determined to put them behind me.

"Everything is fine, Grant," I said. My investigation into Ben's murder must remain a secret for a while. Grant, I felt, would not approve of it.

"It's nice that you are close again, Darcy," he went on, "but be careful. I'm working on finding out who killed Ben Ventris, but so far it's a no-go, and bad as I hate to think it, you might be in danger. Everybody in town knows you and Miss Flora are the ones who found Ben. The killer might think you know more about his death than you do."

"I realize that, Grant," I said. "Thanks for being concerned but Mom and I are okay. We'll call if anything scares us."

"Promise?" he asked.

"Promise."

As I hurried down the front steps to my car, I glimpsed a dark blue vehicle disappearing around the corner. Could that be Ray Drake in his Buick? Why would he be lurking about? Perhaps I should have told Grant about Drake's visit. But the day was too beautiful to let my suspicions spoil it. Backing out of the driveway, I pointed the car out of town.

Turning onto the road toward the river, I glanced in my rearview mirror. That same blue car was following at a safe distance. Were two people in the front seat and was the car really Ray Drake's? Just to be on the safe side, I would do my best to lose him. Instead of going southeast, I headed west, then pulled a quick turn onto a narrow paved lane. Braking, I eased behind a thicket of sumac that bordered the road. From my hiding place, I watched the Buick creep past, Ray Drake at the wheel. He had a passenger but I could not see clearly enough to determine whether it was a man or woman.

Fear rose in my throat with a metallic taste. How dare this man stalk me? And why? He must know something about the gold, but how did he know it? Tales of buried treasure abounded but those old stories had been around for a long time, and why should Ray Drake connect my mother or me with the story of Ben's hidden gold?

Anger replaced my fear. Nobody knew the back roads of Ventris County like a person who had grown up here. Nobody from out of town, as Ray Drake evidently was, would have heard about a shortcut to Granny Grace's old home place.

Putting my car in gear, I drove back onto the pavement. If Drake could follow old wagon roads and rocky creek beds, more power to him!

After winding my way around tree-covered hills and across spring-fed streams, I turned onto the dirt lane that led to my grandmother's land. Below me stretched part of the lake that was formed when the U.S. government dammed Ventris River sixty years ago. My parents used to talk about how the free-flowing river looked in the days before the dam—a different channel and different depths. At that time, the fertile river bottomland grew wonderful crops, but one of the hazards had been flooding. Sometimes water covered a whole season's worth of corn, and all my grandparents' hard work went for nothing.

Now that the land near the river belonged to the government, access to our own acres was harder. Straddling a sagging, rusty fence, I walked downhill toward a creek that splashed through land that was once Granny Grace's and now belonged to my mother.

Mom had told me some months ago about a rancher farther up the creek who had dammed the stream for his own use. Of course, that slowed the creek to a trickle and made it harder for farmers who depended on it for their cattle.

The scent of water, damp earth, and wildflowers mingled with a fragrance I could only call the essence of springtime. Filling my lungs with the fresh air, I thought of one of my favorite Scriptures from the fifth chapter of the Book of Job: "*For you shall be in league with the stones of the field; and the beasts of the field shall be at peace with you.*" That was my feeling about this beautiful chunk of nature.

One of the many dreams that died with Jake was of someday building a house on these acres that had belonged to Granny Grace. We would have retired here and enjoyed our sunset years in my ancestral home.

Tears sprang to my eyes. "Oh, Jake, where are you now?" I whispered. "Heaven is so very far away."

A hard knot of grief began in my chest and spread throughout my body. I lifted my face to the sky and screamed, "Why?"

As the echoes of my voice bounced from hill to hill, I heard a muffled, hoarse exclamation and a splash. Running in the direction of the sound, I pulled branches apart, jumped over briers and there, in the deepest part of the creek stood a large young man. He was in waist-high water, in a still pool under a bluff that jutted out like a prominent nose. Startled eyes jerked in my direction and his mouth dropped open.

"I'm sorry I scared you," I said. "Were you noodling for fish?"

Without a word, he scrambled downstream, splashing water and slipping on rocks until he gained a foothold on the bank. Out he clambered and galloped over the hill.

Had I sounded that frightening? I wished this boy had let me explain. I didn't object to his noodling, even if he was trespassing. Dad told me about noodling, how he had tried it once, feeling under rocks in the creek for fish. Nearly putting his hand on a cottonmouth snake instead of a fish cured his desire to noodle.

Shrugging, I walked upstream, on the lookout for any possible hiding places that might contain the fabled gold. The creek separated my grandmother's land from the farm of Ben Ventris. Through the years, the stream had cut different channels and neither it nor the Ventris River followed the paths they once took. Sycamore trees towered along the creek, some as high as 160 feet. During the days when Ben's ancestors walked Ventris County, those trees would have been much smaller. Did one of them contain a hollow where a treasure could be tucked away? Caves, some small and some large, pockmarked the bluffs. Did one of them harbor a trove of Georgia gold?

Something fanned past my shoulder followed by a loud zing and a pop. Holding my breath, I froze. Another crack, and dirt sprayed in front of my feet. Gunshots! Someone was shooting at me!

Dropping to the earth, I lay there, my heart fluttering like the leaves overhead. Two bullets from an unseen gunman had come chillingly close. I pressed my face into the mossy ground and tried to pray. All I could remember were the words, "Psalm Ninety-one." I whispered this phrase again and again. The rest of the Psalm had vanished from my memory.

Would the hidden gunman shoot again? Could he see me through the trees? Minutes ticked by while I lay frozen in place, afraid to breathe, my ears straining for the sound of approaching footsteps. Would he find me and shoot me point blank?

After what seemed like years, I decided I could not lie here forever, or at least I hoped I would not lie here forever. Maybe the shooter thought he had hit me and I was dead.

In the distance a crow cawed, and from a nearby tree a blue-jay scolded. The sounds of nature were returning to normal. Hopefully, that meant the gunman was gone.

Cautiously, I raised my head and looked around. Nothing moved except the creek and the leaves. I eased up to my knees then stood. Expecting each moment to hear another shot, I trotted downstream until reaching the sagging fence and my Passport, parked on the roadside. Scrambling over the wire, I yanked open my car door and, with a hand that shook badly, turned on the ignition.

"Thank You, Lord," I breathed. Dust and rocks flew under the tires as I stomped the accelerator.

I hadn't wanted to tell Grant about Ray Drake or the trip to New York or what Mom knew about the gold. Now, I had no choice. What if it had been Mom instead of me that the cowardly person had tried to kill? And, if the would-be assassin was Ray Drake, how did he know where to find me? Not many people ventured this far out of Levi on unpaved roads. I had felt certain that no one had followed me, but I was wrong. For the first time in my life, I wished a patrolman would stop me for speeding as I barreled down the road back to the safety of Levi.

CHAPTER 7

Feeling like a child who is forced to confess a misdeed to her parents, I walked into Sheriff Grant Hendley's office.

His receptionist looked up from her computer. "Yes?"

"Is Grant in?" I asked. "I really need to talk to him. I'm Darcy Campbell."

The receptionist's hazel eyes lit up. She evidently had heard about me, which gave me a qualm or two.

The only spot of color in this small space was the bouquet of fresh flowers on the desk of—I squinted at her nameplate—Doris Elroy. Otherwise, the room seemed drab, with brown paneled walls.

Grant opened the door to his inner office before Doris could answer me. Jim Clendon peered over his shoulder.

Swallowing, I said, "Grant, um, I need to talk to you. Alone."

The deputy frowned and stalked through the receptionist's cubicle and out the door.

Smiling, Grant said, "Come in, Darcy." He indicated a heavy, wood chair that faced his desk. "Have a seat."

I sat and drew a long breath. "Somebody just shot at me."

Grant's smile vanished. "What? Who? Where?"

So, I began my story with Ray Drake's visit, progressed to my trip to New York, and finished with the gunman at my grandmother's place on the river.

For a long moment after I finished my recitation, Grant sat silently. At last, he asked, "Are you sure you are all right? Did he hurt you in any way?"

I shook my head.

Grant leaned toward me. "Do you think this Ray Drake fellow is the one who shot at you? It sounds to me, Darcy, like he came too close for it to be anything but attempted murder. My question is why he would want you dead?"

Someone would want to murder me? To hear it spoken sent a chill down my back.

Grant's blue eyes narrowed and a muscle along his jawline twitched. "What else are you not telling me, Darcy?"

Looking down at my hands, I asked, "What makes you think there is something else?"

"Darcy Tucker . . ." he began.

"Campbell," I corrected him.

"Darcy Tucker Campbell, when I talked to you this morning, you said everything was fine. That was an out-and-out lie. Don't you trust me anymore?"

My face felt hot. "Sure. Of course I trust you, Grant, but I wouldn't trust your deputy any farther than I could throw him. Besides, I didn't want to worry you."

Grant's voice was soft but he spoke as if he were biting off each word. "I already explained about Jim. Now answer me. What else should I know?"

So I told him what Mom had said about the gold and the legend of the cache, hidden somewhere in Ventris County.

Pushing his chair away from his desk, Grant swiveled around to gaze at the maple outside of his window. "I've heard about that gold all my life, but I never put much stock in it. Maybe there's something to that old story after all."

He turned back and faced me. "I'll have a couple of deputies watch your place, twenty-four/seven. Whoever shot at you must know by now that he missed, and it stands to reason he's going to try again."

I shook my head. "I don't want you to do that. Mom would probably distract your man by bringing him coffee and apple pie and she would worry that he was too hot or too cold. Besides, I know how to shoot and I can take care of myself. Mom too."

"Like you did today?" Grant asked.

"Okay, but today I wasn't expecting anybody to follow me. Besides, I surprised a young fellow who was noodling for fish. Maybe he was the shooter."

"What'd he look like?"

"He was young, in his early twenties, I'd guess, blond and heavyset. He seemed very shy and ran off when I tried to talk to him."

"That sounds like Jasper Harris, Pat Harris' boy. Jasper doesn't have a job and likes to prowl through the woods and along the creek. I don't think he would harm a flea. He's not quite right; or, maybe he's just different than most of us and we're the ones who aren't quite right in his eyes. No, I can almost swear that Jasper Harris didn't shoot at you."

Pat Harris was the secretary/treasurer of Goshen Cemetery's governing board. She and Mom had several phone discussions about putting the cemetery in shape for Decoration. I remembered seeing Jasper years ago as a shy little boy, but hadn't recognized him all grown up. But if Jasper wasn't the shooter and Ray Drake hadn't been able to follow me, who had shot at me?

Pushing my chair back, I stood up. I shoved my hands into the pockets of my jeans so Grant couldn't see they were trembling.

"Thanks for listening, Grant. I promise to be more careful. Mom will be fit to be tied, but I'll have to tell her about this so she can be watchful. She's entirely too trusting."

Grant walked to the door with me. "I'm glad you decided to let me in on your investigation," he said, "but don't withhold any more information that might be helpful in solving Ben's murder. That's actually a crime, Miss Tucker-Campbell. We still haven't found Ben's body. Someone, maybe the killer, for some reason, took him away and hid him. A person who would do such a thing is unpredictable and dangerous."

"And maybe he's the person who shot at me?" I asked.

He cocked an eyebrow and crossed his arms. It was time to leave. Grant didn't have any more answers than I did. In addition to trying to solve a murder and find a body, he now had two meddling women to worry about.

Driving home, weary with the day's events, the realization of how nearly death had touched me brought tears to my eyes. Promising myself that from now on I would be cautious and suspicious, I, nevertheless, was more determined than ever to find out what was going on in Ventris County. Solving this murder was the only way my mother and I could be truly safe.

CHAPTER 8

How does one tell a parent that her child has been shot at? I tried to break the news to my mother gently, but wound up just blurting out the fact that I had come perilously close to death on Granny Grace's acres.

She listened in silence but her complexion grew visibly paler, and when I finished my story she got up from her chair, came around to where I was sitting, and hugged me. Her voice trembling, she asked, "Could it have been some hunter shooting at rabbits or squirrels?"

I shook my head. Sparing her worry was important, but she needed to know that the person or persons we were dealing with was dangerous and she should put her eternal faith in human nature aside.

Wiping her eyes, she said, "Oh, Darcy, this is all my fault. I wanted you to come back home and you have had nothing but danger since you got here. You could be safe and sound in Dallas now instead of worried that somebody is going to shoot you."

"No, Mom, that's not true. This stuff would have happened, but I wouldn't have been here to help you. You would have found Ben out there at Goshen whether I was with you or not. And Ray Drake would still think that Ben told you the hiding place of that unlucky gold."

"There's no such thing as luck, Darcy," Mom said automatically. All my life she had reminded me that belief in luck was superstitious and Christians were to have nothing to do with it. She went to the cabinet and pulled the coffee canister off a shelf. To her way of thinking, in all times of stress, coffee helped.

"Did you talk Grant out of sending us bodyguards?" she asked as she measured coffee and water.

"I think so. We will just have to be aware of everything and everyone that's a little out of the ordinary. From now on, wherever one of us goes, so goes the other. I don't think it's safe to leave you alone again, Mom."

"Seems to me I wasn't the one who got shot at," my mother retorted. "I should be the one in danger since supposedly Ben told me about the gold, not you. I just can't figure out why anybody would shoot at you."

"Maybe the bad guy thinks that you told me where the gold is hidden or maybe he just wants to scare you into being cooperative because you fear for my safety," I said.

The only sound in the kitchen for the next few seconds was the old yellow coffee pot working its magic. At last, Mom stopped pleating her place mat and smiled. "I have an idea! We'll just take a trip, a short vacation to somewhere or other, maybe back to Bet in Fayetteville."

Getting up from the table, I took two cups from the cabinet. "No, that's not far enough. We'd only put Aunt Bet in danger too. If Drake is watching us, we should go farther than Fayetteville."

"Well, where, then? Timbuktu? Honolulu?"

Pouring steaming coffee into our cups, I said, "Sounds good to me."

Mom paused with her cup almost to her lips. "Is Grant any closer to finding the murderer?"

"He didn't say. He was too busy being mad at me to say anything else. He wants us to stay out of any investigation, but I don't know how to do that. We are not asking to be involved; we just are."

"Darcy, I think the only way we are ever going to be safe again is for that killer to be brought to justice."

"I agree. But how long is that going to take?"

Mom gazed at the rose bush outside her kitchen window. "I keep thinking about the antiques dealer in Oklahoma City, Jason Allred. I'm wondering if Ben went to see him and maybe told him where the gold is. Do you think Mr. Allred could be so greedy that he killed Ben, in order to recover the gold for himself?"

That was an angle I hadn't thought of. "It seems unlikely. Dealers in antiquities are used to priceless items. Integrity and discretion are their stock and trade."

"But what if we talk to Mr. Allred, and find out what Ben told him? Now that Ben is dead, I don't think Allred would be sworn to secrecy, would he?"

I put down my cup. "And you want us to go see Allred."

Mom smiled. "I like Oklahoma City. That would be a mini-vacation. We could stay for several days, and maybe while we're gone Grant will arrest the killer and find Ben's body and get this whole thing cleared up!"

Catching some of her enthusiasm, I said, "If we could leave before daylight, Drake wouldn't know we were gone. He has to sleep some time, just like normal people! And we would be together so I could keep an eye on you. Let's pack tonight and leave bright and early in the morning."

"Good idea," Mom agreed.

Sunrise was only a rosy promise in the soft, gray east when we drove out of Levi the next morning. Mom and I were in a holiday mood. Maybe the trip out of town, seeing different sights, having lunch in a nice restaurant, would be good for her. She had looked tired since finding Ben's body. Leaving Levi with its dark secrets behind us was a relief.

We headed west. The sky was cloudless and promised a perfect day. A niggling memory of another day that began much like this one passed, like a shadow, through my mind. The day we found Ben started out sunny and warm too, full of promise. Mom had predicted a storm the morning we left for Goshen, but the weather had seemed to belie that and I hadn't believed her. Glancing at my mother, I asked, "You don't have any warnings or premonitions this morning, do you? Any aches and pains in arthritic joints?"

She wrinkled her nose. "Not a one! Besides, I listened to the weather forecast last night and rain isn't predicted."

Her confidence reassured me. This little jaunt would be what we both needed. People were already stirring in the farms and ranches we passed. What would their morning chores be, I wondered. What particular defeats or victories would fill the days of the strangers along the way?

Each person was a walking story with his or her own personal tragedies and hopes. The surface of life often masked triumphs or hurts that casual observers never knew. As for Mom and me, we were trying to restore normalcy into our world that had come smack up against an ancient secret. The horror of finding Ben would forever haunt us. Sometimes Mom would pause in the middle of mixing cornbread or pulling clothes out of the dryer and stare out the window as though she were looking fifty years into the past.

The busyness of chores helped the daytime hours pass, but often my nights were restless with worrisome dreams that I couldn't remember the next morning. For some reason, I kept thinking of a phrase that an officer in the Dallas criminal investigation division liked to repeat: "Murder without an obvious motive always comes in threes." Maybe I remembered it because I had often heard my Cherokee grandmother, Grace, repeat something like it: "When a couple of bad things happen, I always dread the next news. Trouble seems to come in threes."

Shaking my head, I tried to dispel thoughts of Ben's murder, the disappearance of his body, and his amputated finger. Perhaps they had been the three occurrences of bad luck.

Mom had more color in her cheeks this morning. Even if we didn't learn a thing from Jason Allred, the trip was going to be good for her.

Slowing down to watch a spring calf frolic in a pasture, I asked, "Would you tell me more about this Hammer person? I don't know anything about him. Did you say he's Ben's nephew?"

Her expression changed and I wished I had said nothing about Hammer. Evidently, he was not a subject that brought any joy.

"Actually, he's not any real relation to Ben. Hammer's mother worked for Ben's brother Sam at one time. They lived far out in the country so there was no doctor and no birth certificate when Hammer was born. About the time he started to school, Sam helped the boy's mother get some identification for him and evidently let him use the Ventris name. Ben always said the boy was bright and energetic. I'm not sure how he got the name 'Hammer.' A nickname, I suppose. His real name was Elijah."

Pulling into the passing lane, I went around a truck with a trailer load of cattle probably bound for an auction down the road.

"So, what happened to Hammer after he grew up? Is he still in Levi?"

Mom frowned. "Seems to me he went up north some place. Hammer was a rotten apple by the time he was a teenager, arrested for theft and for breaking into people's houses, and I don't know what else. Darcy, let's not even talk of unpleasant things today. Look at that! Twin colts!" She pointed out the window.

Smiling, I agreed. "It's a deal. I won't say another word unless it's positive, cheerful, uplifting, and . . . ."

"Oh, hush," she said, smiling once again.

We rode on in silence. I looked forward to meeting Jason Allred. Arlen Templeton said Allred would help me understand the mystery surrounding Ben's gold. I could hardly wait to talk to the man.

At last, Mom spoke. "I hope all this trouble won't affect the way you feel about Levi, Darcy. I want it to always be home to you."

A lump rose in my throat. Home used to be wherever Jake was, but that was in the past. I came back to Levi to heal. Being with my mother was part of that healing. "It always will be, Mom," I promised, "if you are there."

The hours passed swiftly and neither of us said any more about Ben or his gold. Traffic increased as we neared Oklahoma City.

"This place is certainly bustling," I said. "I haven't been here for several years and I'm sure there've been lots of changes. According to my map, Jason Allred's antiquities shop is on a short street near Bricktown."

Mom smacked her lips. "Good! The Spaghetti Warehouse is in Bricktown. We should go there for lunch."

She was the navigator as we drove into the heavy traffic of downtown. With Mom reading the map and street signs, driving was easier. However, I breathed a sigh of relief when I saw a vacant parking place.

Getting out of my Passport, I stretched. "Here we are, capital of the great Sooner State, home of oil wells, cowboys, Indians, and lots of history."

"We hope it holds some answers for us today," Mom added.

A horse-drawn carriage clattered down the brick street. "Is that your preferred mode of transportation?" I asked. "Or would you rather take a pedicab or a trolley?"

"Let's just walk," she said. "I need to stretch these kinks out of my legs."

"It's still early, so why don't we find Mr. Allred first and then go to the Spaghetti Warehouse later?"

"Sounds good," Mom agreed. "The river walk is beautiful! Look at all these lovely flowers and these old, old bricks. With so much beauty in the world, why do people ever take it into their heads to deal out misery and death to others?"

I had no answer. The stores we passed held many intriguing items, but our quest involved one certain shop. At last, I saw it.

Taking Mom's arm, I said, "There's Mr. Allred's, wedged between those buildings."

We stood outside Allred's Antiquities like children in front of a candy store. Everything about it, except the size, spoke of elegance, from the burnished brass lettering on the door to the sample of antiques displayed in the window.

"There's something odd," I said. "The sign says 'Open' but the store is dark. Maybe the inside lighting is dim or maybe we're looking at a corridor leading to the main gallery."

Putting her hand on the doorknob, Mom gently pushed. "The door isn't locked," she said. "I guess that means it's all right to go inside."

As we stepped onto the deep carpet of the shop, a musical tinkle announced our arrival. However, no one hurried to meet us. No sound at all came to my ears except the ticking of a mahogany clock in the entryway.

CHAPTER 9

Silence hung heavy in the plush room; not even the noise of traffic invaded this citadel of antiquity. The walls must have been heavily insulated and the effect was of entering a realm of near-reverence. Mr. Allred's place of business reminded me of another edifice of my childhood —the old Carnegie Library. One always spoke in whispers there and the feeling was the same, even to the musty odor.

Three small lights glowed in the panel above a small desk in the foyer, showing that the security system was on and functioning.

Sunlight filtering through the storefront window did little to relieve the gloom, and nothing at all to displace an air-conditioned chill.

"Mom," I whispered, "I don't like this."

"Neither do I," she said. "That sign outside says the store opens at 10:00 but it's a quarter after that now. Surely someone is here."

Certainly the proprietor or a sales clerk should have hurried to meet us. Businesses that display items in the window with a $2,000 price tag usually are not left unguarded and the door unlocked, even with a security system in place.

When my eyes adjusted to the gloom, I saw something that raised goose bumps on my arms. A glossy, cherry wood display case lay toppled on its face on the floor in a scattering of broken glass. A long necklace of colored stones hung crazily across the back of a chair.

The odor of mustiness grew stronger; yet, it was more than just the smell of old wood and books. It was heavy and acrid. Had Jason Allred become ill before leaving his shop? Perhaps he had started to lock up, stumbled against the display case, and vomited before he passed out?

"Is there a light switch in the entryway?" I asked Mom.

I heard her hand sweeping against the wall and then light from several chandeliers flooded the store. My breath caught in my throat. The tumbled display case was only the tip of the iceberg. This long, beautiful room looked as if a tornado had whipped through. Tables and desks lay on their sides. Shards of broken dishes littered the floor. Paintings had been ripped out of their frames.

Instead of immediately calling the police, as I should have done, my reporter's instinct kicked in. Who had wrought this havoc and why? Was it a wanton act of vandalism? Had a fight occurred between Jason Allred and an assailant? Evidently the object was not theft. Although I was no expert, I knew that many of the items in the shop would bring a bundle if sold in the right market.

I jumped when Mom touched my arm. "Let's go, Darcy," she said. "Let's get out of here and then call 911. I don't want to be involved in any more trouble."

I shook my head. "No, Mom, we can't go yet. What if Mr. Allred is here? What if he needs help?"

Tiptoeing through broken glass, I saw an open door halfway down a hall which connected to the showroom.

"I'm going to check that room," I said, pointing to the doorway.

When I peered inside the small room, I saw that it was an office, but it was in as bad a shape as the rest of the shop. File folders and manila envelopes spilled onto the floor. An empty spot on the desk showed where a computer once sat. The destruction was so complete that a front-end loader could not have done a more thorough job of demolition.

Mom clung to my arm as we crept into the office. Again she whispered, "Come on, Darcy, let's call the police."

Briefly, I wondered why she was whispering. Evidently, we were the only ones in this ransacked shop. The building had an empty feel.

"Wait here, Mom," I said. "I want to see if there's anything in this office to give us a clue about what has happened."

As I inched toward the desk, the acrid smell grew stronger. Dim overhead lights cast an unnatural, orange glow over the wreckage.

I saw the puddle first, so dark it resembled grease in the gloom. Then, a man's shoe came into view on the floor near the desk, a shiny, black loafer. My heart hammering, I moved closer. Dressed in a suit and stretched out on his side on the floor lay the body of a man. Around and under his head pooled the source of the pungent smell. He lay in blood, and I had the sinking feeling that I had found Jason Allred.

Steeling myself against rising nausea, I bent over that pitiful figure and felt his wrist for a pulse. He was cold and I could detect no flicker of life. An open billfold beside his hand identified him as Jason Allred, but something caught my eye just as I was about to get to my feet. A small gold chain glittered between two buttons of Allred's shirt.

Mom grabbed my shoulder. "For heaven's sake, Darcy! What are you doing? Don't touch that poor man! Don't you know what they say on TV? You're going to have your fingerprints all over. Maybe the killer is still here. Let's leave! Now!"

Carefully, I undid a button near the chain. A narrow leather belt was buckled around the dead man's chest and another strap extended over his shoulder. The belt ran through slots in a long velvet pouch. Gently, I pulled the chain and a medallion slipped out of the pouch into my hand, the same medallion as in the photograph in Templeton's office in New York.

Mom and I stared at each other in horror. So this is what happened to Ben's heirloom. Jason Allred would never divulge any secret Ben may have told him. My mother and I had arrived too late.

55

CHAPTER 10

It was mid-afternoon before Mom and I had lunch at the Spaghetti Warehouse, but even then neither of us felt hungry. After the police arrived at Allred's shop they questioned us extensively, both there and at precinct headquarters. I debated whether I should hand over the medallion to the police, but Mom persuaded me that it was the right thing to do. However, that involved going into depth about the background of the medallion and Ben's murder. Finally, the investigating officer called Grant to verify our story. Grant must have done some fast talking to keep us from being detained. At any rate, our trip to escape a killer in Ventris County and clear our minds of past sad events had failed miserably.

"Do you think the person who killed Mr. Allred is the same one who killed Ben?" Mom asked, taking a sip of icy sweet tea.

"I would say that it is a strong possibility. I don't know how the killer learned about Jason Allred, but there has to be a connection. He must have been hunting for the medallion and Allred refused to give him any information. Maybe Allred was killed to keep him from identifying his killer. I would guess that something scared off the murderer before he searched Mr. Allred's body. Oh, I don't know, Mom. I'm just trying to figure all this out."

A horrifying suspicion caused me to choke on my tea. I knew for sure that someone was watching me—possibly Ray Drake—as I had seen his car slide past my hiding place when I was on the way to Granny Grace's. Had he or someone else followed me to New York City? Had he been in the plane during my flight? Had he tailed me through the labyrinth of city streets to Arlen Templeton's office? Fishing in my purse, I pulled my cell phone out and found the number for Forrestal Antiquities. Punching it in, I waited as it rang in that far off office.

"Who are you calling?" Mom asked.

I held up one finger. "I'll tell you in a minute."

The brittle voice of Minda Stilley answered on the first ring.

I identified myself but before I could tell her the reason for my call, she laughed and said, "Oh, Mrs. Campbell, I'm so glad to talk to you again. One of your concerned law officers from Levi dropped in after you left the office. He said he is keeping an eye on you and wanted to be sure you stayed safe. He wanted to know where you planned to go next. Wasn't that thoughtful? Mr. Templeton was out of his office but I found that paper on his desk with the address of the Oklahoma City antiquities dealer. Of course, I want to aid the law in every way I can and most certainly thought it was nice of him to be watching over you, like a guardian angel."

A cold hand seemed to close around my throat. Shutting my eyes, I waited for a moment before I could find my voice. It was just possible that Ms. Stilley's helpfulness had cost a man his life.

"Can you remember what the law officer looked like?" I asked.

She giggled. "Cute. He kept his cowboy hat on the whole time, but he had dark hair and a nice tan. Very attractive. I wouldn't mind having somebody like that watching over me."

Thanking her, I hung up. Cute? Surely that let out Ray Drake. A lawman? Was it Jim Clendon or somebody with a fake ID?

Mom's voice betrayed her anxiety. "Why did you call that New York antiquities dealer, Darcy? Why are you looking like that?"

Shaking my head, I said, "I'm afraid that Mr. Allred's death just got more complicated." And I reiterated Minda Stilley's information.

Mom was silent for a long while, gently stirring the ice in her glass. At last, she said, "We may as well go home tomorrow. I sure don't have the heart to sight-see and evidently we are just as safe in Levi as we would be here."

I nodded. "You're right. Thank goodness the chief gave us permission to leave. Since he had us write down our life history, he probably feels it's safe enough to let us go."

When we arrived back in Levi the next evening, the telephone's message light was blinking. I pushed the play button and heard Grant's voice.

"Darcy, when you get home, give me a call either at the office or at my house. I've found out something about Ray Drake that you should know."

It was after six o'clock, so I found Grant's home phone number and punched it in.

"Thanks for helping us get out of the city," I said. "If you hadn't talked to Chief Spencer, we'd probably be locked up by now."

"I doubt that," Grant said. "I did some checking on this Drake character and that isn't his real name. He's a long way from being an FBI agent, and the blue Buick he drives is a rental car. Drake is actually Cub Mathers. It was a long route to trace him down through papers he filled out for the car agency but he rented it in Houston, flew there from Chicago, and then drove up here. That's a roundabout way to get to Oklahoma, but he probably had other fish to fry along the way. Anyhow, Cub is a big-time crook in Chicago. He's officially known as a hit man."

"A hit man?" I gulped.

"Yep. You and Miss Flora entertained one of the most heartless guys in Illinois. There's not much he wouldn't do. Like it or not, I'm sending a patrol car by your house every hour. Leave all your outside lights on so my man can have a good look as he passes, and Darcy —"

"Yes?"

"Darcy, be careful. I think trouble follows you like a hound dog follows the trail of a raccoon. When did you get to be such a magnet for danger?"

"Hey! Thanks for comparing me to raccoons and hounds. I'm not a magnet for anything, thank you! This is your quiet, peaceful town, Mr. Hendley. May I remind you that I'm not the sheriff here?"

As I hung up, I heard him chuckle. He irritated me so that I forgot to tell him what I learned from Minda Stilley.

Sleep eluded me that night. Tomorrow was the long-awaited Decoration Day at Goshen Cemetery. Mom and I would get up early, load the car with flowers, and return to the cemetery. Neither of us had been there since the day we found Ben's body.

Somewhere in the darkness, an owl hooted. Crossing to my bedroom's double window, I peered out. Perhaps I could glimpse my favorite bird. I didn't believe the ancient superstition about owls announcing trouble. Hearing an owl could mean there would be a change in the weather. That wasn't superstition; that was fact. Again, the owl hooted softly.

Another superstition haunted me, the one about trouble coming in threes. First was Ben's death, then the Oklahoma City antiques dealer. If I believed that old saying, there'd be one more death. Superstitions surely did not belong in a civilized society. "Fear is the opposite of faith," I told the invisible owl.

Nevertheless, someone was responsible for the murders. Allred's death must surely be tied to Ben's, but enough of such thoughts! A cup of hot tea would relax me.

As I turned from the window, something moved at the front corner of the house. My heart did a flip and landed in my mouth. Had the movement been a piece of paper blown by the mounting wind? Or maybe it was just a shadow and my nerves were playing tricks. But, as I squinted into the night, the shadow moved again.

Gripping the windowsill, I forced myself to breathe normally. If someone was lurking around the house, would he try to get in? Should I call Grant or dial 911? If it turned out to be just a cat or a dog looking for scraps of food, I would feel foolish calling the law.

Dad's handgun still lay downstairs in the bookshelf drawer. I would feel better if I had it, just until I could decide what else to do. Mom was sleeping and I didn't want to wake her. Hopefully, she had remembered to lock the outside doors before going to bed. Another thought stopped me on the stairs. Had someone managed to get in while I debated what to do? Was an intruder even now waiting for me in the darkness?

Creeping down the stairs and into the living room, I slid open the bookshelf drawer, lifted out the small gun, and tiptoed into the kitchen. I didn't dare turn on a light. Familiar objects looked alien to me; shadowy shapes that must be the table and chairs could be hiding places for an intruder. A soft scratching sound came from the back door, the rasp of metal on metal. I stopped, paralyzed. Someone was trying to get into the house.

At that moment, a horrible eardrum-splitting noise shattered the stillness. Our neighbor's donkey brayed one long and raucous blast. My nerves snapped. I screamed and heard footsteps running across the back porch. Adrenalin shot through me, blotting out the fear. I wanted to see this person who had dared invade our home. Gripping the gun, I ran to the door and yanked it open. On the other side of the trees, a car started. Tires screeched as it roared away.

"Darcy! Are you all right? What in the world is going on?"

Mom ran into the kitchen as I picked up a scrap of paper wedged between the screen and the door. Slipping it into my pocket, I closed and re-locked the door.

Turning to my mother, I muttered, "Somebody just paid us a visit but the donkey spoiled his surprise."

Mom blinked. "Somebody tried to get into this house?"

"Yes."

The adrenalin evaporated, leaving me feeling as limp as a wet dishrag.

"Oh, what are we going to do?" Mom wailed. We held onto each other and I don't know who was shaking more. "We should call Grant," she added.

"I guess. It won't do any good though. Whoever it was is not here now. We are evidently dealing with an evil person or people, someone who is so sure that we know something about Ben's gold that he is willing to go to any length."

Mom's voice sounded quavery. "The Lord certainly protected us tonight, Darcy."

"Do you mean when the donkey brayed?"

"Yes. I don't remember that it ever brayed in the middle of the night before this. That and your scream scared away the person at the door."

"Then I'm grateful to the Good Lord, Mom. He must hear your prayers."

"He always does," Mom said. "He hears yours too."

I pulled the paper from my pocket. "I found this between the screen and the door." In my palm lay a wrapper from Red Man Chewing Tobacco.

Mom poked it with her finger. "Do you know who chews that brand?"

"I saw Jim Clendon take a package of it from his pocket the day we were at Goshen Cemetery."

We stared at the cellophane wrapper. At last Mom said, "Lots of people chew tobacco and lots of them buy Red Man."

"Yes, but do we want to show it to Grant? In fact, do we want to tell him about this at all? He'd probably move a deputy right into our front room, and who knows if it'd be someone we could trust? Maybe our intruder was the officer who has been driving past our house every hour. Maybe he is Clendon or one of the other deputies."

"I'm bringing some quilts and pillows downstairs," Mom said. "We can leave on all the lights, inside and out, and sleep down here the rest of the night."

"And I'm sleeping with this little fellow," I said, patting the gun. But our plans for sleep were optimistic. We heard a thunderstorm blow in, shower us with rain, and move out. The owl's prediction was right as far as the weather was concerned. Was he also predicting the near break-in? At last, the sun appeared and our long night ended.

CHAPTER 11

Decoration Day dawned as lovely and serene as only a May day in Oklahoma can. Goshen Cemetery basked beneath an early morning sun. Droplets of dew sparkled like emeralds and rubies on freshly-cut grass. Birds sang in ancient cedars, undisturbed by groups of people moving quietly over the cemetery with their bouquets of flowers.

After the long drive from Levi, it was good to get out of my mother's Toyota and stretch. The blue sweater across my shoulders felt welcome because the air was brisk. Unlocking the car's trunk, I pulled out two baskets filled with artificial flowers, then we joined the people who had come to pay their respects to departed loved ones.

Goshen still bore scars of that fierce storm that had roared through. A gaping hole and sawdust marked where the oak had stood. The storage building had not yet been replaced.

A tradition in my family for at least a hundred years, Decoration Day at Goshen always took my thoughts back to how it might have looked to those early day settlers: women in long dresses and bonnets, men carrying their hats which respect demanded they remove from their heads, walking quietly among the headstones. Instead of rows of cars outside the cemetery fence, teams of horses switched flies while they waited, hitched to family wagons. Those wagons carried not only people but tubs covered with dish towels. Under those towels nested fried chicken, biscuits, boiled eggs, and fruit pies. At noon, families would take this food to the creek below the cemetery, spread out quilts or lunch cloths, and share food and conversation. The custom of eating the noon meal at the cemetery did not diminish the sacredness of the day; rather, it was a necessity. Many people traveled miles to get to Goshen and horses and wagons were a lot slower than today's transportation. Sometimes the trip took hours; thus, it was impossible to get back home by lunch time.

Mom and I had a system. With a long screwdriver, I punched a hole in the ground near each headstone and she dropped in the flowers. We decorated my dad's grave first. Remembering Andy Tucker, his laughter, his devotion to Mom and his love for me, I whispered, "I miss you, Daddy," before I moved on to the next resting place.

Jake's grave was in Dallas, his hometown, where his parents still lived. Would I ever have the courage to visit that lonely cemetery again?

"It's good to see you, Flora; you too, Darcy. It must be so hard to come back here after that awful thing about finding Ben." Earlene Crowder came up behind us. If I remembered correctly, this skinny, red-haired woman with curiosity shining in her blue eyes was a second or third cousin of mine.

Earlene's husband, J. Lee, piped up, "The real shocker must have been when ol' Ben just up and disappeared. Bet that about gave you a heart attack, didn't it, Flora?"

"Is that Margie Mullen way over there?" Mom waved to an unsuspecting person on the far side of the cemetery. "Excuse us, folks. I do want to talk to Margie."

"Pretty slick," I told her. "I hope we can dodge other questions that easily. Oh, dear! Here comes Lavina Pugh."

Finally, we quit trying to avoid people and just answered their questions with minimum information. So far, no one knew about Ben's severed finger, and I hoped nobody found out. No one had mentioned hidden gold either, which was a good thing.

We emptied both baskets of the flowers and I glanced at my watch.

"Look at the time! Doesn't the business meeting begin at ten?"

"Yes," Mom said, "and I must be in the chapel to read the minutes from last year. Maybe the meeting won't last long and we can go home pretty soon. I'm tired."

The little stone chapel held memories of the last time we were there, shivering from cold and shock. Who had gone out the back door just as Mom and I entered? Would that person be in the group gathering inside now? Was he the one who killed Ben? Were we rubbing elbows with a murderer? Nervously, I scanned the crowd for Ray Drake, alias Cub Mathers. Surely he would not be seen in public. He must know by now that we were onto his real identity. Taking a deep breath, I sat down beside my mother in the second pew from the front, south side of the aisle.

A movement behind the podium caught my attention as a small gray mouse skittered across the floor. The little rodent was busily catching moths caught in cobwebs along the baseboard and I welcomed the diversion. If I could keep my mind on that mouse, perhaps I could sit in this haunted place with a minimum of stress.

The president of the Goshen Cemetery Board, Hiram (pronounced "Harm") Schuster, stood at the front of the assemblage. He cleared his throat and ran a finger around the collar of his long-sleeved white shirt.

"Folks," Hiram said, "I want to remind you that this meeting will be conducted in decency and order. Some mighty upsettin' things have happened lately on our hallowed grounds, but business must be done anyway. I'd like us to bow our heads and open this gathering with prayer."

"After Hiram's "amen," Patricia Harris led us in all the stanzas of "On Jordan's Stormy Banks." Had Patricia chosen that old hymn randomly? No one needed reminding of the storm that had swept over this historic place and the controversy surrounding Ben's death and disappearance. We sang without the benefit of the rickety upright piano in the corner. By the time we reached the last verse, the song was dragging and I was glad when it ended.

I gave Mom a thumbs up for reassurance as she stood and faced the crowd. She read the happenings of last year's meeting with a clear voice. After she sat down, Patricia Harris gave the financial report.

Someone at the back of the room snorted. "Seems to me there ought to be more than $5,000 in the cemetery's savings account. I thought there was that much last year."

"Why do we keep asking for donations if the cemetery has so much money? And speaking of that, we ought to use it for the cemetery's upkeep, not hoard it." This came from a stooped, white-haired man whose nasal voice did not match his angelic face.

"Say, Pat, weren't you trying to buy some of Ben's land? Now, it's none of my business, but I know I couldn't afford to buy that river bottomland, so how could you?"

I forgot my proper upbringing and turned around to glare at Tom Bill Monroney. What an insult to Patricia. He was right—it was none of his business at all. But in spite of my righteous indignation, I was surprised. I had not known that Pat wanted to buy any of Ben's land, and wondered why she wanted to.

Viola Prender stood up, her black eyes snapping with suspicion. "I make a motion that we choose an independent group to investigate our books. We have had a terrible thing happen in our midst and we want that awful murder of Ben Ventris solved. If it has anything to do with this cemetery, we must hand over all information to Sheriff Hendley."

Patricia Harris sprang to her feet and stared at Viola. Her voice was shaking as badly as her hands. "I have done nothing wrong," she said. "These books are open to the public. What's wrong with you all? Have you lost your senses? You've known my son and me all our lives. You know we are honest. I don't like all these accusations being thrown around."

Hiram pounded on the podium and the gray mouse disappeared into a hole in the baseboard. "Here, here, folks. Let's have some order. We've got cemetery business to take care of and we don't want to go pointing fingers at honest Christian people."

A noise like the roar of an enraged bull interrupted Hiram. The young noodler from my grandmother's acres jumped up beside Patricia, nearly overturning his pew.

"You all had better not go accusin' my mother of doing anything wrong, Tom Bill, nor you either, Miz Prender. You all just shut your mouths!" Jasper Harris reached over a pew, grabbed Tom Bill by the shirt collar, and drew back his fist.

Tom Bill's Adam's apple went up and down a few times. Finally, he squeaked, "I didn't mean nothin', honest, Jasper, I just heard some things, that's all."

Patricia was weakly patting her son's back, telling him to shush. Jasper slammed Tom Bill down and stomped from the building. Patricia scurried after him, sounding like a leaky tire in her attempts to calm her son.

That episode ended the business meeting. Hiram surrendered and sank down on the nearest pew. The buzz of voices reminded me of a nest of angry hornets. Mom and I squeezed through the crowd pouring out of the door. I looked around, trying to see Patricia or Jasper. Glimpsing Patricia's carefully waved gray hair disappearing down the hill near the creek, I turned to my mother. "Let's see if we can catch up with them. I'd like to find out more about their relationship with Ben—gently, of course. I sure wouldn't want to rile Jasper any more than he is."

A piercing scream echoed and re-echoed from the surrounding hills. The hairs on my arms stood up. What or who was that?

When I was able to move, I sprinted toward the creek. Behind me, I heard hurrying footsteps but I outran everyone. The scene before me stopped me in my tracks. Patricia stood at the edge of the small stream, staring at a bundle of clothes that were half in, half out of the water. Her face was whiter than the steppingstones across the creek.

Peering closely at the cause of Patricia's horror, I saw the clothing in the stream contained a body, the body of a woman whose loose black hair washed up and down with the current. Gasping and clamping both hands against my mouth, I closed my eyes.

Mom leaned against me and moaned, "Oh, no! Darcy, it's Ben's daughter. It's Skye!"

Unbelievable and ghastly, but true. Ugly blue bruises showed around the woman's slim neck. Less than a month after we found Ben's body here at Goshen, Skye Ventris had followed her father in violent death.

Skye had lived in Oklahoma City. Jason Allred lived in the same town. Had the killer been unable to get information from Allred and then looked up Skye? Had he committed two murders the same day? And why had the killer brought both Ben and Skye to Goshen Cemetery? What twisted brain thought it was important to do so?

CHAPTER 12

The Monday following Decoration Day was bright and beautiful, but to my mother and me a pall hung over the morning. The death of Skye Ventris was almost beyond comprehension. When Grant, Jim Clendon, and the EMTs arrived at Goshen yesterday, they were grim and suspicious of everyone. Grant questioned Patricia Harris, Tom Bill Monroney, Viola Prender, Hiram Schuster, and Mom and me. They would have talked to Jasper but Pat's son had disappeared. Nobody could find him nor knew where he might have gone, including his mother. Shock and disbelief shone on the faces of everyone at the cemetery, and I didn't see how the killer could have been anyone gathered inside the chapel.

I felt as if I had lost a family member, not that I knew Skye very well, but I had talked to her only a few days ago. Could I have done anything to prevent this? Should I have warned her of possible danger? When I was in Oklahoma City, I could have looked her up, but Allred's death seemingly froze my thinking process.

Mom lifted the lid on a pot of pinto beans simmering on the stove. "I wonder what happened to Jasper?" she asked. "I wonder if he didn't see Skye in that creek before he ran off."

Putting two plates on the table, I asked, "Are you sure he wouldn't become violent enough to kill someone? He really lost his temper with Tom Bill; however, there wasn't enough time between his running out of the chapel and our finding Skye to choke her to death. I suppose he could have killed her before the business meeting."

"I have never seen him angry before today," Mom said. "I think he feels protective of his mother and didn't like what the others were insinuating. I don't know why they suspected Pat of anything. She's as honest as the day is long."

"It's just too bad Jasper ran away," I said.

"I've watched that boy grow up," Mom said. "He sort of withdrew and became a loner. I was surprised to see him at the cemetery yesterday. Other children laughed at him when he was a youngster because he was different, so he stayed to himself. For as long as I've known them, it's always been just Pat and Jasper."

"Maybe he already knew that Skye was dead and he was afraid to tell anyone, afraid he'd be blamed. Maybe that was why he was so ready to take on Tom Bill."

"I don't know . . ." she paused at the sound of a car's horn. "That would be the mailman. Cliff always honks if he has letters for me."

"I'll go check," I said.

The mailbox contained the usual bills and ads and a long, white, official-looking envelope. There was no return address but the cancelled stamp read Oklahoma City.

Wiping her hands on her apron, Mom took the envelopes. She put the bills on the cabinet and the ads in the wastebasket. She pulled a letter from the long, white envelope and gasped. "Why, it's from Skye Ventris. She had to have mailed it only a day or two before she was killed."

In a voice that shook, Mom read aloud, "*Miss Flora and Darcy, here is the map to the treasure that Dad told you about. I don't think you were supposed to have it unless something happened to him. Well, it has happened and I hope he was right in sharing this with you. I'm afraid if word gets out that you have the map, you may be in danger. The map isn't clear and when I come to Levi in a few days, I want to take you and show you where the gold is. It's easier to show than tell you. Something recently caused Dad to worry about his safety. He mentioned his past catching up with him but he wouldn't tell me more. Somebody had come to visit him, somebody who worried him, but he wouldn't say who it was. Anyway, this is the map to the gold. I don't need it. I have it memorized. Since Dad is no longer with us, I thought I should send a copy of his will too. Blessings on both of you, my friends. Skye."*

Mom read the will and sat down suddenly. She handed the papers to me. I skimmed the ancient map. It made no sense to me. Then I glanced at Ben's will and sat down too.

Picking up my glass of iced tea, I pressed it against my hot forehead.

"Unbelievable," I whispered. "Mom, Ben's will states that in the event anything happens to both him and Skye, you are heir to everything he owns."

"I know," she whispered weakly.

Pouring her a glass of sweet tea, I said, "It's too much to take in, especially while we are dealing with Skye's and Ben's deaths. Let's look at the map. Maybe you can recognize some landmarks. I can't."

The paper on which the map was drawn was so old that it was yellow and brittle. The edges crumbled under my touch. Tiny holes and spots pockmarked it.

"I guess those symbols are trees." I pointed to some triangles with stems. "And I suppose these lumpy things could be rocks. That squiggly line is the river, maybe?"

Turning to Mom, I said, "This county is full of trees and rocks. As well as the river, several creeks run through. This map is a puzzle to me. If anyone is smart enough to decipher it, he deserves the gold!"

"Wait, wait," Mom said, pointing at one edge of the old document. "See those letters and numbers at the top? That looks like a land description. Run back and get my mother's abstract to her land. It's in my cedar chest."

For years I had tried to persuade my mother to rent a safety deposit box but she put her trust in the security of that cedar chest. Finding the old abstract, I brought it to her. She opened it, scanned the land description of Granny Grace's acres and then compared them with the faded symbols on the map.

Her eyes shone as she looked at me. "I know where this area is. It joins my mother's land."

"Do you know what that means? The gold must be somewhere just over the line between Ben's farm and Granny's." I swallowed half my glass of tea.

She pointed to the squiggly line. "I don't think that line is the Ventris River. I think it's that little creek between our land and Ben's."

"The creek where I saw Jasper noodling," I said.

Mom turned the map around. "And this extra big triangle must represent an extra-large tree; maybe one of those sycamores."

"Yes, but which one? There are lots of tall sycamores along the creek."

Other faded markings on the ancient paper seemed to be written with the Cherokee syllabary. To decipher them, we'd need an expert in the Cherokee language.

My head began to ache and my mother rubbed her eyes. "Let's take a break," I said. "We can look at this again after lunch."

Going to the stove, I began ladling beans into a brown crockery bowl. "We are going to have to find this gold, whether we want to or not," I said.

Mom pulled a pan of crusty cornbread from the oven. "You're right. Until the gold is found and turned over to the sheriff, that killer is going to be a menace. Maybe after he knows that he can't get his hands on Ben's treasure, we'll be safe."

"And, maybe Grant will nab him," I said, sitting down at the table.

Nobody bakes cornbread like my mother. I buttered a slab and took a bite.

"An alternative to searching for the gold would be to hop a plane to some place far away," I mused.

My mother evidently had changed her mind about taking a trip. "When I let a petty crook run me out of my home, I'll be ready to meet my Maker."

"Poor choice of words, Mom, but I know what you mean. We really must do our best to find that gold. Maybe in finding it we'll also bring Ben's killer to justice."

She nodded. "To me, that's far more important than the gold."

We studied the map for an hour after lunch but were no closer to guessing what it meant. At last, I rubbed my aching back and stood up. "I'm taking a break from this thing and going to my computer. Hopefully, writing down the order of recent events will help me think more clearly."

My mother nodded, but kept gazing at the enigmatic map.

Putting my glass of tea on the floor beside me, I sat down at the computer and typed:

First Event: Ben Ventris's death, disappearance, and finding the missing finger

Second Event: Ray Drake's visit. Drake had lied to us about being an FBI agent; instead, he was part of a bloodthirsty Chicago mob, but how would he know about Ben's gold? Chicago was a long way from Levi.

Third Shocker: Someone shot at me while I was on my grandmother's land. I remembered the bitter taste of fear and my heart catapulting into my throat.

Shivering, I wrote: *The Fourth Occurrence: finding the body of Jason Allred.* Who had gotten to the antique shop ahead of us? Had Allred told the murderer about the gold? If the killer had been looking for the gold medallion, he tore up the whole shop without finding it.

Fifth: Someone tried to break into Mom's house. Neither she nor I had slept well since that night. Mom was evidently a target but why would the murderer want her out of the way? Judging from my close encounter with the shooter, I was a target too.

Again, I wished that Ben had not involved my mother in any of this mystery about hidden gold and sending her a map. Not that the map would do us much good, because we had no idea what it meant. Whether the killer knew about Ben's will or the map, he would probably guess that Ben had confided in her because of their friendship.

This last murder was, to me, even more horrifying: *Shocker Number Six: Patricia Harris found Skye Ventris's body in the creek in back of Goshen Cemetery.*

Now Jasper was missing and if the rumors flying around town were correct, so was Tom Bill. Gossip had it that Jasper may have killed both Skye and Tom Bill but I didn't think so. To my way of thinking, Tom Bill decided it was wise for him to get out of Dodge until Jasper calmed down; however, I could be wrong.

As I stared at the list, I realized something else. Mom and I discovered the first and second murder victims; Patricia Harris found the third one. Mom and Pat both served on the Goshen Cemetery board. Adding to the weirdness was the fact that both Skye and Ben had, in all probability, been killed elsewhere then their bodies taken to Goshen. Allred was left in his shop in Oklahoma City, but the Ventris murders pivoted around a cemetery. This must be significant, but how?

Finishing my glass of tea, I stared at the computer screen without reaching any conclusions. There was one thing I could do to make my mother and me a bit safer. I'd call the only home security business in Levi.

Les Cooper of Watchful Eyes Security assured me that he would come as soon as he could. Since the murders, everybody in town either wanted a security system or a dog. I figured that the electronic watchdog would require less upkeep.

"Can't you come tomorrow?" I asked.

"Sorry, Miss Darcy. I can't do that. But I'll get you all fixed up before the week is done. That much, I can promise."

I returned to the computer—that wonder device. How had I ever managed without it?

Googling "Dahlonega gold" and the "state of Georgia" led me deep into American history. The California gold rush is something every schoolchild learns about, but significant amounts were also mined in northern Georgia. According to one website, Hernando De Soto first visited North Georgia in 1540 because he had heard rumors of gold. Indians who lived along the Chattahoochee River discovered it. Who knew how many years that occurred before De Soto?

By the time the soft spring dusk shaded into night, I felt that I could sleep even if a whole carload of bad guys were camped outside.

I had gone over and over my list of events, and before I turned off the computer I sent out emails to eight colleagues at my Dallas newspaper. I asked whether anyone had any knowledge of legends concerning gold brought into Oklahoma from the east.

Newspaper folk are an odd bunch. There's a lot of pushing and shoving for a good story, but when one of them sends out a call for help, they will come through. Hopefully, I'd get at least one good lead and maybe somebody would be well-versed in the Cherokee language and could decipher that map of Ben's.

My search for information would wait until tomorrow. There was quite a bit of cornbread left from noon. Mom still slept upstairs, so instead of waking her, I heated the cornbread, poured a glass of milk, and sat down to a bedtime snack. Hopefully, tomorrow would hold some answers. Surely it was time for at least a few pieces of the puzzle to start falling into place. I felt as if I were lost in the woods and every turn I made only led me farther in.

CHAPTER 13

Lying in bed that night with the breeze fanning my face, I began to relax. The cool air felt as soothing as my mother's hand when I was a child, sick with a fever. Sighing, I burrowed into my pillow. In younger years, I would repeat Bible verses before going to sleep. What had happened through the years that made me feel God was far away? When my dad died, it hurt terribly, but Mom was there as a buffer between me and death. When Jake died, there was no buffer and the finality hit me head on. Jake had been my rock and he was gone. Would I ever find the peace and trust that I once felt?

I would try, once again, to remember a favorite Scripture. Closing my eyes, I whispered the beginning of Psalm 27: "*The Lord is my light and my salvation; whom shall I fear?*"

Who, indeed, Lord? I thought drowsily, *if You are with me?*

Sleep vanished as a sound penetrated my consciousness. I sat bolt upright. What had awakened me? My bedroom curtain moved as a breeze blew through. Had the wind knocked something off my dresser?

Throwing back the sheets, I padded to the window. The full moon lit the front yard, making it almost as bright as day and throwing long shadows of trees and bushes across the grass. An owl disengaged itself from the moon-silvered oak and flew silently away. Owls are night birds, and sometimes they fly into yards, so there was nothing unusual about seeing it. Maybe it hooted and that was the sound that woke me.

Something, however, felt wrong. Could this be the same owl I heard before our near break-in? Had it adopted Mom and me and taken upon itself the job of guarding us?

As I gazed at the shadows in the yard, one of them moved. This shadow was large and upright. A man stepped out from behind the oak. As if I were watching an old, silent movie, a smaller figure appeared, walking toward the man, her housecoat flapping in the breeze. Mom! That was my mother, alone and unprotected in the middle of the night, closing in on a stalker who had trespassed into the yard!

Panic urged me down the stairs, shoe-less, with not even a robe around my pajamas. Yanking open the front door, I dashed toward those two moonlit figures.

"Mom!" I yelled. "Get away from him!"

My mother turned toward me and spoke in a quiet voice. "It's all right, Darcy. This is Jasper Harris. I think he is hungry and needs to come inside for a sandwich."

Five minutes later, I sat across from Jasper at the kitchen table, watching him wolf down bread and cheese, a slab of apple pie, and a glass of milk.

Mom put a cup of coffee in front of me before sitting down. We must have made a strange tableau: two silent women staring at this young giant, his elbows keeping his chin off the table. The only sounds in the kitchen were Jasper chewing and then his satisfied, "Ahh" as he drained the glass of milk and pushed back his plate.

He grinned. "Thanks, Miss Flora."

Mom patted his hand. "I remember when I taught you in Bible School. You were always the best eater at refreshment time."

I could stand the charade no longer. "Is it just me or does anyone consider this situation to be a tad odd? If it doesn't hurt your feelings, Jasper, will you kindly tell me what you were doing skulking around our yard at one o'clock in the morning?"

Fear shone in Jasper's eyes. He squirmed in his chair.

"Now, now, Darcy," soothed Mom. "Did you know that everyone in town is worried about you, young man?" She smiled at our visitor.

"Maybe you would like to tell us where you've been. If you are in trouble, Darcy and I will do our best to help you."

I set my mug onto the table with a bang. "We will?"

To my dismay, Jasper's mouth crumpled like a child's. Tears ran down his face. "You was always nice to Ma and me, Miss Flora. You and Ben treated us real good. I ain't never forgot that. Ben even brought us groceries once when Ma's check was late. It hurt me that somebody killed good ol' Ben and left him out there in that pile of sticks and rocks and even cut off his finger."

The sound of the old wind-up clock over the sink seemed as loud as a snare drum. Outside the kitchen window, the wind made little skirling sounds as it blew around the corner. I opened my mouth but no words came out. Mom's eyes sent me a message. She wanted me to let her ask the questions. We must not alarm our guest who, after delivering such astounding news, seemed poised to get up from his chair and disappear into the darkness.

Leaning toward Jasper, Mom said, matter-of-factly, "So you saw Ben in that pile of dirt and sticks at the cemetery. You saw that his finger was missing."

Jasper nodded. "Ben had helped us and I wanted to help him. I couldn't leave him out in the storm, now could I?"

Numbly, I shook my head.

Jasper nodded and looked down at his empty plate. "So, I took him off to a place where he can sleep and nobody will bother him."

Faintly, Mom said, "You wanted to give him a decent burial. Of course you did."

"I didn't bury him exactly," Jasper confided, "but Ben is where he'd want to be."

Ignoring my mother's warning look, I said, "What do you mean, you didn't bury him exactly?"

Jasper's face settled into stubborn lines. He scooted his chair away from the table. "I ain't sayin' anything more. Where Ben is, that's my business. I know he'd want to be there and that's all that matters.

Nobody knows where he is except me. The owl and me. We're the only two knowin' Ben's whereabouts and that's the way it's going to stay."

This thing about owls was beginning to get under my skin. "Do you mean that owl that was in the tree where you were hiding tonight, Jasper? Is he your pet?"

Jasper looked smug. "That's for me to know," he muttered.

Mom quickly rose and poured Jasper another glass of milk. "And what about Tom Bill? Do you know where he is?"

"Ol' Tom Bill? Why, no. Is he gone somewhere?"

Mom shrugged. "He probably is just on a little trip," she said. "Maybe he'll turn up soon."

I leaned toward Jasper and tried to speak as gently as Mom had. "Where were you Saturday night? Did you come to our house then?"

Jasper looked at me pityingly. "Sometimes I can't sleep. Then I go walking. I just walk, no place in particular. Saturday night I was in the woods behind your house and I saw somebody right up against your house. I was slipping up on him, keeping an eye on him. I couldn't figure out why anybody would come around at that time of night. He snuck around and climbed up on your porch. I was just about to collar him when that ol' donkey brayed! Ain't never heard anything so awful in all my life. I guess it scared him 'cause he ran off. I watched for a while longer to make sure he wasn't comin' back."

If Jasper could be believed, he wasn't our intruder that night. Mom said the Lord kept us safe. Not only had He caused the donkey to bray, He had sent Jasper to guard us.

Shifting in my chair, I said, "Getting back to Ben, Jasper. It's important that you tell Sheriff Hendley where you put him. Do you know anything about Skye Ventris? You know she's dead too, don't you?"

Jasper's eyes widened. "No! No way am I goin' to talk to the law. They'd think I killed Ben and Skye too. They'd lock me up. Uh-uh. Nobody's going to lock me up and nobody's going to find me or Ben neither!"

Jasper shoved back his chair and bolted out the back door.

I ran after him. "Wait! Wait! Jasper, you've got to tell us. You won't have to talk to Grant."

Mom shook her head. "He's gone, Darcy."

Locking the door, I returned to my chair. "Yes, he's gone back to hiding. But Mom, at least now we know how Ben disappeared from the cemetery. And Jasper is big enough that he could have moved Ben by himself."

I closed my eyes, trying to not see an image of a frightened boy who, in spite of the lightning and rain, cared enough about his friend to move him out of the storm. Jasper had meant to do a good thing, but he had only complicated this mystery and perhaps brought trouble upon himself.

Gazing at Mom, I asked, "Do you think we'll ever get a full night's sleep?

Sighing, Mom said, "I can only hope. Somehow, it's reassuring to know that somewhere out there, Jasper is keeping an eye on things. We don't need a security system, Darcy. We've got the Lord and Jasper Harris."

CHAPTER 14

Somewhere during the rest of that dream-riddled night, I reached an inescapable conclusion: Ben's hidden treasure was the reason for all these bad things happening, and Mom and I had no choice but to find it—the sooner the better. If we turned it over to the authorities, surely we'd be rid of anyone who had evil designs upon our lives.

Peering at the bleary dial of my bedside clock, I decided that I might as well use these early morning hours to work on my article for *The Dallas Morning News*. My editor would be calling to ask why I hadn't emailed him the story. Since Ben's death, everything, including writing, had been pushed to the back burner. Not only did I feel I could write about the impact of rural technology, I felt very well qualified to do an article for the American Medical Association, titled, "Sleeplessness and Finding Dead People Speeds Up the Aging Process."

Stumbling down to the kitchen, I measured coffee and water into the yellow pot and turned it on. As I waited for that first perfect cup, I went to my computer. Within seconds, information flashed onto the screen concerning Georgia gold. I learned that the dome of Atlanta's capital was gilded in gold leaf. That was most surely due to the first gold rush, in Georgia.

I continued reading, finding that no significant gold mining goes on in Georgia today.

The only reference I found to explain the greenish cast of Dahlonega gold was speculation from a geologist who said that although it is impossible to duplicate conditions Mother Nature originally planned for northern Georgia, he believed that veins of gold crisscrossed veins of silver when the two were forming. These two metals mixed with clay and humus, which may have caused the unusual shade of yellow in that particular gold.

All this information, while interesting, didn't help in our search for the killer in our midst or point me toward the hiding spot for Ben's cache.

What about the map? How could I find out what it really meant? Was the gold still in the same place as when the map was made?

Taking a sip of coffee, I felt it burn all the way down, a definite eye-opener. While I was panting for air, Mom came into the living room.

"Did you find anything interesting?" she asked.

"I'll leave it all up onscreen and you can read it later. What are we going to do about Jasper's visit? Do you think he was telling the truth, that he was the one who moved Ben?"

"No reason to doubt it," Mom said.

"We should call Grant and tell him that if he can find Jasper, maybe he can make him tell where Ben's body is."

"Do you really think we should, Darcy? That boy is scared to death that Grant will lock him up and he'll never tell anybody what he knows. Besides, I don't think involving Jasper any more than he is would help us find the hidden treasure or the killer who's still on the loose."

Thinking about the implications of this, I wondered what would be the legal term for keeping quiet about Jasper's late night visit. Aiding and abetting? Obstructing justice? Mom believed in the creed of the hills: keep your mouth shut.

"If Grant ever finds out that we . . ." I began.

She interrupted. "How's your coffee, Darcy?"

"Good, fine," I answered. "And very hot."

"I'll pour a cup then start breakfast. How would Grant find out? I don't think anybody but Jasper and you and I know what Jasper told us."

I shook my head and clicked on my emails. Evidently, one of my colleagues had sent my request for information on to somebody else. This message was from a stranger, a Bess Alberts. She wrote, "*Hi, Darcy Campbell. You have a nationally known expert on local legends and languages living almost in your backyard. Her name is Emma James and she taught here at Boston University for more than thirty years and has had several books published on your subject of interest. She is now retired and lives in the little town of Uvalda, Oklahoma. I can't even find it on a map, but it must be near you. Her address is 270 Thayer Avenue, Uvalda.*"

Could she help us in deciphering Ben's map? There was only one way to find out.

"Mom," I called, "How would you like to take a trip to Uvalda?"

After a breakfast of oatmeal, toast, orange juice, and coffee, my mother and I got into my Passport and headed out of town. She had gotten Emma James's telephone number by dialing 411. Miss James asked us to come for a visit and said she'd be happy to help if she could.

Following my navigator's instructions, I drove west out of Levi and turned onto a narrow, paved road that wound through tall oaks and sycamores. Grass and wildflowers bordered the asphalt. A bird of an amazing shade of blue-green flew across in front of us.

"This is lovely country," I said, "but I wonder why anybody with an advanced education degree would leave a big city like Boston to retire in such an out-of-the-way place like Uvalda?"

"Maybe her roots are here," Mom said. "Maybe she just came home. Your dad and I used to buy apples and sweet potatoes from a man who lived in Uvalda. I think the population then was 150 or so. I doubt that it has grown much. Some people just prefer small towns."

Grinning at her, I said, "And then again, there are some of us who like the bright lights of a big city like Levi."

"There's nothing wrong with Levi," Mom muttered.

A small sign beside the road welcomed us to Uvalda, population 200. I would say that qualified as a small town. My mother was right, Uvalda hadn't grown much.

On Main Street, a lot of buildings appeared deserted. The Wagon Wheel Restaurant was evidently the center of town. Half a dozen cars and farm trucks were parked in front of the entrance. A sign proclaimed, "Today's Special: Two eggs, sausage, biscuits and gravy, only $2.99."

My hearty breakfast of two hours ago suddenly didn't seem adequate. My stomach growled. I could almost eat again.

Uvalda's Main Street also boasted a small grocery store, gas station, and two antique shops.

Mom peered at the instructions Emma James had given her.

"Turn here at Grove Street. It intersects Thayer Avenue."

Miss James lived in what was undoubtedly the fanciest structure in town. A sweeping front porch supported by graceful columns welcomed us to a yellow, two-story, Southern-style house. Everything looked freshly painted, even the shiny black weather vane atop the garage. A brand new four-wheel drive Jeep Cherokee sat in the driveway. Evidently, this woman did not intend to be homebound by a howling Oklahoma snowstorm.

Emma was on her hands and knees in a flowerbed surrounded by gardening tools and attended by two yellow-striped cats. In spite of wearing a white tee shirt, faded jeans, and a big straw hat decorated with daisies, she looked as elegant as she had sounded on the phone. Her hair was partly silvery gray and partly ash blond, too streaky to have come from a bottle. Even her long, slender bare feet added to her aura of grace. She rose hastily and brushed dirt off the knees of her jeans.

"Oh, my goodness," she said. "I'll bet you are the women who called this morning. I'm so sorry. I didn't realize time was getting away from me. But then, I never do when I'm working in my flowers."

Striding to the corner of the house, she turned on a water faucet, and washed mud off her feet, smiling and apologizing all the while. Drying on an old towel, she slipped into brown leather sandals.

"Please, come in," she said, holding wide the screen door.

The lovely living room was cool and light. Emma's home displayed mementoes of many different cultures. A walnut highboy and matching chest shone with the patina of age and loving care. Even I, an antiques ignoramus, could tell these pieces of furniture were of French design from the past century. A big, southwestern tapestry adorned the far wall and a glass display case held a collection of what seemed to be Aztec decorative items. While our hostess went into the kitchen for iced tea, I wandered to the bookshelf and read the titles of some of the volumes that lined one whole wall. Two leather-bound books caught my eye: *Legends of Old Settlers* and *Ancient Wisdom*. Both were written by Emma James.

Returning with a tray carrying a cut glass pitcher and three matching glasses, she murmured, "Sun tea. It's the only way to go."

Emma sat on a mauve and silver striped loveseat, crossed her legs, and cradled a frosty glass between both hands. "Now, how can I help you?" she asked.

During the drive to Uvalda, I had pondered that very thing. So many questions crowded my mind that I didn't know where to begin. The simplest way would be to tell her what we knew and just let her reach her own conclusions.

Glancing at Mom for encouragement, I said, "First, I'd like you to look at this." I handed Emma the ancient map which I had slipped inside a plastic document cover.

Emma read the map, turning it every way and even slanting it toward the window to get more light.

Shaking her head, she said, "I'm sorry. I really can't tell you much about it. It's a map made by somebody who knew nothing at all about land boundaries and it is very old. I can only guess that the map is supposed to mark the spot for something important. These land descriptions at the top probably were added long after the map was originally drawn. This," she said, tapping the plastic cover, "may represent a tree and this odd symbol, although part of it has crumbled away, I believe is the word 'owl' written in the Cherokee syllabary."

My mother gasped and I felt my scalp prickle.

"Emma smiled. "Yes, owl, *wa-hu-hi*. I'm sure you know that some people are superstitious about owls. They are thought to presage major events."

Actually, this was not what I wanted to hear. Already I had had more experience with owls than I ever wanted to have. "We know about that superstition," I said, "but it is hard to accept that anybody would take this seriously nowadays. Perhaps people believed it long ago before they knew about Christianity. Ben Ventris, the man who was killed a short time ago, believed in Jesus and went to church."

Unbidden, came the memories of the owl's call the night of the attempted break-in, the owl in the tree in our front yard and again when Jasper paid us a visit, and that strange thing Jasper said about an owl knowing where he put Ben. Unaccountably, I felt cold.

Emma James nodded. "This map was probably made a very long time ago, Darcy. Back in the years before Christian missionaries entered the lives of olden cultures, aboriginal people had a different belief system. True, the missionaries did a remarkable work. The Cherokee people are an enlightened, forward-thinking group. As one of the Civilized Tribes, they had a highly developed culture. I'm not saying that your Ben Ventris believed in any of these superstitions, I'm just saying that 'owl' is the word on this map." She handed the document back to me. "Now, let's hear the rest of your story."

As I began my unbelievable tale of murder, mayhem, and mystery, I knew I was doing a bumbling job of telling it. I had to backtrack and start over a couple of times. Re-living all that had happened and trying to put everything in chronological order made me feel a bit queasy. It was a good thing, after all, that we hadn't stopped at the Wagon Wheel for that greasy breakfast.

Touching my arm, Mom broke into my tale. "We feel sure that Ben's daughter was killed for the same reason Ben was killed; probably, that antiques dealer in Oklahoma City too. But, for now anyway, law enforcement just doesn't seem to be getting to the bottom of things."

Emma shook her head. "No. I can see that."

One of the yellow striped cats slipped into the living room and leapt up on her lap. She stroked its shiny fur, her forehead creased in thought.

At last, Emma spoke. "All three deaths are, of course, related, and, in my opinion, there is but one murderer."

"That's what we think," Mom interjected.

Recovering my enthusiasm, I added, "The gold medallion that I found on Jason Allred proves that the murderer, at least, hadn't found it. I don't know if he was looking for it or for information about the hidden gold he thought Ben had given Allred."

"Maybe both," Emma said.

I nodded. "The Oklahoma City police said there was no evidence of a robbery. To my way of thinking, the killer wanted badly to know the location of Ben's hidden treasure and Minda Stilley may have given him the directions to Mr. Allred."

"And, Mr. Jason Allred would not tell his killer what the man came to find out, the location of the hidden gold. That is, if he actually knew," murmured our hostess.

Again, Emma seemed lost in thought, as if she were seeing the violent person who laid the shop to shambles and killed its owner.

Finally, she spoke. "Yes, these deaths are all tied together, all by the same person. Anything else would be just too much of a coincidence to be coincidental. The man who is behind these murders is extremely violent and will stop at nothing to attain that gold."

A nice phrase, that, "too much of a coincidence to be coincidental."

Emma gently placed the cat on the floor. "This equation has one common denominator—the stash of gold. Somebody knows just enough about it to believe it exists, whether it does or not. Didn't you tell me that Ben bought some oil lands several years ago?"

I nodded. "He gave them to his daughter."

"Perhaps he used the gold for that," Emma went on. "Or perhaps there is more gold. Anyway, this person who wants it, as I said, is desperate and has already killed three people. By the way, I hope you two know that he wouldn't hesitate to add more victims to his list, if he found it necessary."

My mouth felt suddenly dry. I took a sip of tea.

Emma placed her glass on the tray. "And this map you brought is supposed to point the way to buried treasure."

"Yes," Mom and I said together.

Next, Emma launched into what would have been a very effective classroom delivery, if we had been students. "Over the ages, every culture has produced many legends of hidden treasure. In most cases, that's truly what they are—just legends. But the story surrounding this sounds authentic. Maybe there is truly a hidden cache that one or more of Ben's ancestors brought when he or she came to Indian Territory. Evidently, our killer believes this is true. But he hasn't seen your map, I hope."

I hesitated. "I hope not. I'll bet, though, that he knows there is a map somewhere. Maybe that's what he's most interested in. Maybe Ben wouldn't give it to him and Ben was killed for being so stubborn. Same for Skye and Jason Allred. The topography along the creek and river has changed a lot in recent years. Without a map, I don't think anyone could begin to locate a certain spot that might or might not contain gold. But this map is so vague that I don't think it's much good. There are hundreds of trees and rocks and one pretty much looks like the other."

"Yes," agreed Emma, "but your killer might not know that. He just may know that somewhere, there's a map. Now, let's see how that affects the rest of your problem."

Grabbing a small notebook and a pen from my purse, I proceeded to take notes.

"Many early people had some rather unusual beliefs and customs about death," Emma told us, looking from Mom to me. "One of the strangest was the idea that the spirit lingered after it left the body. Some thought that a body must be buried in a proper place with a proper ceremony in order for the spirit to gain entrance into another world. Yet, although that belief is similar to what about half the world's population believes, it's really quite different in this point: the spirit was thought to be capable of doing actual harm to a living person; especially if that person had anything to do with the deceased's death."

So the murderer could be in trouble? He might be haunted by the person he had killed? What a strange, new possibility.

"So," I said, thinking aloud, "if the killer believed this, he would want to make sure that Ben and Skye were disposed of in a manner that wouldn't bring their spirits back to haunt him?"

"Uh-huh," Emma said.

How silly that anybody should believe such a horrible thing! Is that where the idea of ghosts and haunts came from? How awful it must be, to be governed by such superstitions. But then, on the positive side, a person who believed this might be a little more cautious about taking the life of another.

Chewing on the end of my pencil, I asked, "But why dump them in Goshen? That is a little far-fetched, even for a superstitious killer. Would it fit the bill for a proper place for the killer to dispose of his victims?"

Emma cleared her throat. "Actually, yes. He would consider the cemetery to be hallowed ground."

I forgot note-taking as Emma continued. "I think you will have to believe that the killer is someone who knows about these old beliefs and is still governed by them. Maybe his conscience is not quite seared over and he is counting on the fact that he put Ben and Skye in a sacred place to outweigh the fact that he is guilty of murder. I'm sure that he tries to justify what he has done, maybe he thinks he needs the gold worse than they did. I would guess that, in some strange way, he is trying to absolve his conscience."

"Wait a minute." I dropped my pencil and notebook back into my purse. "This killer knows the old beliefs, knows about the story that Ben's family might have brought some gold out of Georgia and buried it somewhere. I would say he knows an awfully lot about the Ventris family."

Emma nodded. "It does sound like it."

Mom shook her head. "Ben didn't have anybody else except his daughter. I know that for a fact. And he didn't have any sisters, just a brother. His brother Sam didn't have any children. Of course, Sam let that boy, Hammer, use his name, but he wasn't related. I also know that Ben couldn't have any more children after Skye because, as an adult, he had mumps, and that took care of that! When Skye died, she was the last of the Ventris family."

Emma looked intently at my mother. "Are you sure Ben had no other children?"

Mom snorted. "Of course he didn't. He and his wife only had Skye."

Emma surprised me by chuckling. "And you are positive? I know that Ben was a good man, but sometimes temptation hits us when we least expect it and, before we know it, we've done something completely out of character."

My mother said not a word. Her face paled and she looked as if she were going to faint.

I took the glass of tea out of her hand. "Mom, are you all right?" I asked.

Emma James reached out to her. "Would you like some water? An aspirin?"

Mom's reply was a hoarse whisper. Her mind seemed somewhere else. "The winter after I married Andy, that's when he got the flu and it turned into pneumonia. That was before Ben got married."

"Who, Mom? Did Dad get sick?" How strange that she should revert to talking about my father in the middle of a conversation that had nothing at all to do with him.

"No, no, not Andy. It was Ben. Ben got the flu and then pneumonia."

My mind was whirling, trying to follow what she said. Should we persuade her to go lie down? Should I call a doctor?

But her next words let know that her problem wasn't physical. When she next spoke, I had to strain to hear her. "Ben got sick and couldn't get up and take care of himself for a long time. As I said, he wasn't married at the time. That's when his brother sent the girl who was staying with him over to help Ben. Her Cherokee name was Spotted Fawn, but I think she was known as Ella. Anyway, I thought at the time . . . I mean, I had the feeling that . . . ." Her words trailed away.

I took her hand. "Yes? So she took care of Ben while he was sick. But, I don't understand, Mom. What does it mean?"

She refocused and looked at me in the same way she did when I was a teenager and she was explaining why certain things were off limits for me.

"You still don't understand, do you, Darcy? Spotted Fawn was Hammer's mother. That much we already knew. Hammer was born less than a year after she stayed at Ben's house, taking care of him while he was sick. Darcy, that young man who grew up to be a bad apple might actually be Ben's son."

Words failed me. If that were true, then certain things began to make sense. Emma looked intently at my mother and then at me.

Reaching for her glass of tea, Mom quickly took a sip then set it back on the tray. "I just never made that connection until now. Looking back, I remember Hammer's eyes; the same shape and color as Ben's. The shape of his nose, I can see that there could be a resemblance."

Emma nodded. "Such things happen."

I reached for my purse. "We're jumping to conclusions here which might not be true. Growing up with Sam, Hammer would still have heard something about that legend of gold. And, why couldn't his father have been Sam?"

"It stands to reason . . ." Mom began. "Emma, we've taken up enough of your time. Thank you. You have certainly given us something to think about."

"I wish I could have done more," Emma said. "That map is ancient and the topography of the area has changed since the dam went in. Much of it is covered by water. But meeting you both has been a joy. You've brightened my day. Please come again."

Neither of us said a word on the drive back until we reached the outskirts of Levi.

"Talk about not seeing the forest for the trees," I said. "We've got to look at this from a different angle. Maybe Grant should be looking for Hammer instead of Drake."

"Somehow, I just can't believe that Hammer is related to Ben," Mom said. "He is just too different. Ben was a good man; honest, upstanding. Maybe Sam was Hammer's real father. Wouldn't Ben have known that Hammer was his son?"

"I don't know. Would he? Would Ella have wanted him to know? Is Ella Spotted Fawn still alive?"

"No, she isn't," Mom said. "I remember when she died. It was when Hammer was in grade school."

"So he grew up with Ben's brother, Sam?"

Mom nodded.

"Maybe Hammer felt that nobody wanted him," I mused. "Maybe he got into trouble because he was acting out his feelings of rejection."

"And maybe you took too many psychology courses in school, Darcy. We all make choices in this life. Hammer made a lot of wrong ones."

My mother, the lenient one, so kind to Jasper, sure wasn't cutting Hammer any slack. That was another facet of her character that I hadn't known. Time and circumstance bring out characteristics that perhaps none of us know we possess.

CHAPTER 15

After the drive to Uvalda and the visit with Emma, exercise sounded like a good idea. I hoped that increased blood flow and a fresh supply of oxygen would clear my brain of all but the essential facts, the pertinent parts of this mystery. Slipping on my oldest, most faded blue jeans, and a red T-shirt, I went to the storage shed behind the house. I pulled out Mom's gardening gloves, a spade, and some snippers. Taking a page from Emma James's playbook, I hadn't bothered with shoes. The grass felt cool and comfortable under my bare feet.

A few weeds dared to raise their heads among the peonies by the front gate. That would never do! Getting down on my knees, I began pulling up those offensive upstarts, and before long, the pile of weeds had grown to a respectable height. My muscles complained about the sudden exercise, the sun was as relaxing as a heat lamp as it beat down on my back and head, and I felt a nap coming on. I deserved it! Leaning back against the fence under the peonies, I closed my eyes.

I slept and dreamed. In my dream, the fragrance of flowers surrounded me and I stood by the gate, watching someone walk up the street toward me. I knew the figure was a man, but I could not see his face clearly; however, I certainly welcomed him and couldn't wait for him to reach me. The person must be Jake, I decided. Jake had come back to me. At that moment, the gate squeaked and a voice spoke. My dream evaporated like a mist.

"Hello, Sleeping Beauty."

My eyes popped open and I saw scuffed brown cowboy boots. My gaze traveled upward over snug blue jeans and a short-sleeved blue-checked shirt, to a smiling face topped by a white Stetson hat.

Shading my eyes, I said the first thing that popped into my mind. "Oh! You're not Jake."

Grant's smile disappeared. "Sorry to disappoint you."

Squirming uncomfortably, I glanced down at my bare feet sticking out in front of me. Dirt smudged my arms, but it was too late to run into the house and wash up. I must look a sight.

"Grant, you didn't disappoint me. Um, I mean . . . I didn't know you were coming."

His grin returned. "I didn't mean to disturb you. You look relaxed."

Had my mouth hung open in my sleep? Had I drooled? Quickly wiping my face, I realized too late that I still wore Mom's dirty gardening gloves.

"Don't get up," Grant said. "I'll sit here on the grass. I just wanted to talk to you or Miss Flora about these murders. I can talk as well out here as in the house."

He dropped his hat to the ground, and sat facing me. To my disgust, my heart began to beat faster. What a shallow person I must be. Jake had not been gone a year and here I was feeling drawn to an old flame. I scooted back to put some distance between us.

Grant broke off a grass stem and absentmindedly rubbed it between his fingers. "Have you had any more encounters with bad guys? Any prowlers? Any suspicious people hanging around?"

Jasper Harris popped to mind, but Mom and I had decided to keep his moonlit visit to ourselves. Jasper couldn't really be considered a prowler. He wasn't prowling, just lurking.

"Darcy?"

"Prowlers," I repeated. "No. No prowlers. We have a new burglar alarm system. That makes us feel safer."

Grant flipped the blade of grass toward the sidewalk. "Glad to hear it. You would have called if anything had happened to scare you. Right?"

"Sure. You can count on that. Thankfully, we've been comparatively fright-free."

Never had I seen anybody with more piercing blue eyes than Grant Hendley. They seemed to probe my guilty thoughts. Quietly, he asked, "So, what's going on, Darcy?"

Had he seen into the depths of my secretive soul? Did he know that I was being a little less than honest?

"I don't think I know what you mean, Grant," I muttered.

"Sure you do. I remember you well, Darcy. I have never met anybody who is as nosy as you are. If there's something you don't understand, you won't be happy until you ferret it out. You'd never be any good at playing poker."

Nosy? Curiosity and a healthy interest in seeking the truth should never be misconstrued. This man could irritate me like no other.

"I don't remember that you were quite so blunt when we were in high school, Grant. Didn't that law education include a class in diplomacy? Ferret out? Aren't ferrets those sneaky little weasels?"

He actually laughed. "Now, don't get your back up, Darcy. I just want to be sure you're telling me everything you know about Ben's death and that so-called cache of gold. You've been poking around, and don't deny it. You wouldn't be you, if you didn't. I'd sure hate to think, though, that you're withholding information and obstructing justice."

Knowing that my eyes squinched up and my forehead wrinkled when I frowned, I frowned anyway. "So, are you going to haul me off to jail, Sheriff?"

Chuckling, he said, "Now that would be just plain silly, wouldn't it? No, I'm just wondering if you've glimpsed Ray Drake, the person the good folk in Chicago call Cub Mathers. He seems to have disappeared off the face of the earth."

"If I had seen him, believe me, you'd be the first to know. People like Drake seem to have a short life span and lots of enemies. Maybe one of them got to him."

"That's possible. I've been asking around the county and I found out some things about Ben that I didn't know. Would never have guessed, in fact. You haven't seen any strangers, have you?"

Emma James had mentioned coincidences. Seeing a suspicious stranger around Levi at this time would be too coincidental.

"No," I answered. "Nobody except Drake. But then, you remember, I've been away for a good many years."

Grant was silent for a moment, finding something interesting in the top of the oak. "I don't suppose you've heard tell of Jasper? I just came from his mother's house. She swears that she has no idea where he is."

"If anybody knows Jasper's whereabouts, it should be Pat. Mom says they are close," I evaded.

Grant reached over and wiped a fleck of dirt off my nose then he stood and dusted off his jeans. I stood too.

Glancing at the peonies, he broke off a stem. "I hope Miss Flora won't mind if I take this with me. I've always had a soft spot for that pretty bush."

He climbed into his white Ford Ranger. With a wave in my direction, he drove off down the street. For some reason, the sun's brightness seemed to dim.

"Was that Grant?" Mom called from the front porch.

Walking slowly toward her, I said, "One and the same."

"Has he found out who killed Ben?"

"No," I said. "He asked if we knew anything that could help him solve these murders. I hate keeping secrets, Mom. I should have told him about Jasper and I should have told him about the map and Ben's will."

Drawing a deep breath, Mom said, "If it worries you, Darcy, go ahead and tell him."

I shook my head. "No. It's too late now. I don't want him to know I've kept things back."

Mom's face registered surprise. "Darcy! I didn't know you felt that way. We aren't lying; we just aren't volunteering information."

"Maybe," I said, climbing the steps to the porch. "Would you like for me to help you with supper?"

She turned to go back into the house. "No. We're just having vegetable soup and it's almost ready."

While my mother was occupied in the kitchen, there was a little chore I needed to do. Going to the telephone in the living room, I dialed a familiar number.

CHAPTER 16

My mother was really mad at me. Her reaction to Emma James revelation had alarmed me and I insisted that she see a doctor. While she was busy with supper the night before, I made an appointment for her. She was not happy about it and insisted she felt fine. The victory I won was probably a Pyrrhic one.

Dr. Richard McCauley stuck a tongue depressor into my mother's mouth just as she mumbled something.

He pulled out the depressor. "What did you say, Flora?"

Mom snorted. "I said that I'm here only because of my stubborn daughter. There's nothing wrong with me."

Dr. McCauley smiled and proceeded to examine her.

When the doctor pressed the stethoscope against her chest, Mom threw me a sideways glance that would have shriveled a turnip.

The doctor wound the blood pressure cuff around her arm, for the second time, and she wouldn't even look in my direction.

Shaking his head, Dr. McCauley said, "Your blood pressure is way up. Let's see . . . ."

He thumbed back through her file. "It usually runs low, in the neighborhood of 110/60 but today it is 150/90 and that's too high."

Dr. McCauley pulled a stool toward him with his foot, sat down and observed her over the top of his glasses. "Now, why don't you tell me what's worrying you?"

Crossing her arms over her chest, Mom snorted again. I put a hand over my mouth to stifle a giggle. She was beginning to sound like a steam engine.

"Nothing is worrying me, any more than what's worrying most people," she said. "You're the doctor. Why don't you tell me what you think is wrong?"

Dr. McCauley had dealt with my mother for more than twenty years. Tapping her hand lightly, he said, "I'm betting the problem with you, Flora, is finding Ben Ventris like you did and then later his daughter turning up dead over there in Goshen Cemetery. It's no wonder to me that you are stressed. Any normal person would be."

She nodded in my direction. "Well, then, you ought to examine Darcy too."

He nodded. "I'll be happy to do that. And I bet neither of you has been sleeping well. Isn't that right?"

Years of experience had produced acute discernment in Dr. McCauley.

"No, I'm fine, Doctor," I said.

The truth was that both Mom and I were uneasy because we feared a return visit from someone poking around in our yard at night. Jasper might be keeping watch and that new burglar alarm was in place, but wires could be cut and Jasper's roaming through the woods was erratic.

Although Dr. McCauley was a sympathetic listener, I balked at telling him all this. He might think we were just foolish women with a wild imagination.

"Everything else checks out okay, Flora," the doctor continued. "But you need to keep an eye on your blood pressure. Do you have a monitor at home?"

"She doesn't, but I'll get one," I promised.

"Fine. I'll give you a prescription for these new sleeping pills that I guarantee will work." Speaking to me, he said, "I think you should both try them. They aren't habit forming."

Although I nodded in agreement, I had no intention of taking those pills. Perhaps Mom would use them. I didn't like taking anything that slowed down my mental processes, and somebody should be aware of what was going on around our house each night. I just wished Mom would realize I was worried about her health and had insisted on the doctor for her own good.

Apparently, Dr. McCauley sensed the tension between us and thought he'd help out. "Now Flora," he said, "your daughter was right in bringing you here to see me. We don't want a recurrence of that problem you had last year with an irregular heartbeat, do we? Keeping an eye on your blood pressure is the smart thing to do. You know, sometimes we're so used to being independent that we have a hard time figuring out what's best for us. I think that's one reason the good Lord gave us children."

He winked at me behind her back. "You've never had a weight problem, your bones are remarkably strong, your lungs sound like those of a thirty-year old, and you don't even need glasses except for reading. If I didn't know better, I'd swear you hadn't reached the ripe old age of sixty. You're in much better health than a lot of women your age. We want to keep it that way."

As he talked, he scribbled on a prescription pad. He tore off a sheet and handed it to me. "I wonder, since neither of you is tied down with a job right now, if it might be a good idea to get away for a while. Go down to Florida or take a cruise; something like that." He patted Mom's shoulder. "Then by the time you get back, maybe the sheriff will have caught Ben's killer, and you'll have nothing more to worry about."

A short while ago, Mom wanted to do just that—maybe not go to Florida, but she wanted us to leave town for safety's sake. If we were going on a vacation, I would vote for Georgia. I'd like to visit the land that produced the metal which caused men to lie and kill. But my mother's enthusiasm for a vacation had vanished after we got Ben's will and the map. And then, of course, Skye Ventris was killed. In some strange way, these events put a new determination into my mother. Since she was the only person standing between the killer and the treasure, a normal person might want to keep a low profile; not Mom. Now she was determined to stay in Levi and not be run out of her home.

Now, she was just plain angry. She reminded me of a tiny chipmunk who once faced up to our family cat. Mom had a stubborn streak a mile wide. If I was blessed with stubbornness too, I needn't wonder where it came from.

Mom looked the doctor in the eye. "You can quit this 'we' business and patting me and talking to me as if I were a three-year-old, Richard McCauley. You are certainly old enough to know that running away doesn't solve anything and I am certainly old enough to make my own decisions."

Dr. McCauley raised his eyebrows, but he made no further comment. As we got back into my Passport, I thought I'd try and break the ice.

"Looks like we both need to keep an eye on our blood pressure," I said.

Mom did not reply. Neither did she say a word to me all the way home.

My mother believed in cooking or cleaning to relieve stress so immediately after lunch (a very quiet affair) she hauled out the furniture polish, mop bucket, mop, Windex, and a wad of paper towels.

Jerking her head toward the hall, she said, "You can clean the bathrooms."

I made sure she didn't see my grin. She knew I didn't like cleaning bathrooms and she gave me that job because she was still irritated. I knew her well enough to realize there was no sense in trying to talk to her until she got over her snit, so I took the mop, bucket, and Windex and dutifully went upstairs to the hall bathroom.

CHAPTER 17

I scrubbed and cleaned and was beginning to polish the windows when I glanced out at a car which certainly looked out of place in Levi, Oklahoma. It was a late model, silver BMW convertible, and it turned into our driveway. I tried to keep from salivating. What a beautiful automobile.

The man who stepped out of the car looked as out of place in our town as did his BMW. He wore stylishly flared burgundy trousers and a silvery sport coat the same shade as his car. A pale pink shirt completed his ensemble.

The stranger carried a shiny briefcase with a clasp that caught the afternoon sun. He came to the bottom step of the porch, paused, then reached down and wiped the dust off his loafers. Grandpa George's voice echoed from my childhood: "Never trust a man who wears a suit and girly shoes." From where I stood, I guessed those shoes were made from the hide of some hapless alligator.

I ran downstairs.

The man stepped back when I opened the wood door; the storm door stayed firmly latched.

In a soft voice and flashing movie-star white teeth, he asked, "Mrs. Campbell?"

Before I could reply, he held up a business card. "I am J. Smith Rowley. I am an attorney representing a client interested in Ben Ventris and his estate."

"Huh?" I asked just as Mom came up behind me.

Frowning at him, she asked, "Who? Who did you say you represent?"

Smiling, he said, "I don't believe I said, Ma'am. May I come in?"

J. Smith Rowley's colorless eyes seemed to slide everywhere. When he realized that we were about to refuse to let him in, he hurriedly added, "I have a document here that I think you'll be interesting in seeing."

Mom unlatched the storm door. We stood aside for him to enter but, once again, I stayed close to my dad's hidden gun in the bookcase.

Sitting down on the sofa without being invited, J. Smith Rowley snapped open his briefcase and placed it on the floor. A diamond ring on his finger looked as if it cost more than my mother's house.

Mom sat in her rocker facing our visitor while I stood against the bookcase. If I had anything to say about it, this man was going back out the door as quickly as he came in. He had better talk fast.

Rowley cleared his throat. "I am here as the legal representative of an heir of Benjamin W. Ventris and, as such, I have the authority to speak on my client's behalf."

Interesting information, this. "Please go on," I said.

"I have here a petition that I am prepared to file, asking that the court appoint me as representative of the estate for Mr. Ventris's true heir. Due to the fact that Mr. Ventris died intestate and . . . ."

"Wait a minute. 'Intestate'?" Mom asked, looking at the lawyer as if he had just crawled out of a crack in the corner of the room.

Before Mr. Rowley could open his mouth, I said, "It just means that Ben died without a will." Frowning at my parent, I briefly shook my head, hoping she wouldn't say anything about the will Skye sent.

The lawyer nodded. "Actually, my purpose in coming is to ask you two ladies to help the proceedings move along by signing a document for me."

We waited.

The smile that flitted across his narrow face was oily enough to grease wagon wheels. "This is a very unusual situation because, although we all know that poor Mr. Ben Ventris is dead, there was never a death certificate since the (ahem) body disappeared before the medical examiner could arrive on the scene. So, because of that horrible circumstance—and what a shock it must have been, dear ladies . . . . " He gave us a look that I guessed was meant to be sympathetic. "The judge will require that we have a signed statement from both of you to present to the court, along with this petition from the heir as proof that the deceased is actually dead. It's just a small, gracious gesture that will help expedite things."

My mother smiled sweetly. "What makes you think we'd want to be gracious?"

Mr. Rowley's eyebrows drew down. So did his mouth. "I am certain, when you stop to consider, you'll realize that it is the only thing to do. As responsible members of society, you'll want to do everything possible to see that Mr. Ventris's property is handled in the way he would have wanted."

If J. Smith Rowley had said "gullible" instead of "responsible" members of society, it would have described his evident opinion of us.

Stepping toward him, I said, "That goes without saying. May I see the petition that names the 'true heir' as you put it?"

Rowley raised his eyebrows. "Please, Mrs. Campbell, you should know that I can't divulge that."

"I know nothing of the sort," I said.

Mom crossed her arms over her chest. "You are wanting us to buy a pig in a poke, Mr. Rowley."

"A pig in a . . . that's quaint, Mrs. Tucker. No, what I need are your signatures and then I'll be running along. Won't take a minute."

As he spoke, he pulled an official-looking document backed in heavy gray paper from his briefcase. "I'll be happy to notarize your statements right now so you won't even have to make a trip to the bank for a notary public."

"And what if we don't choose to do that?" I asked.

Rowley's tone became threatening. He half-closed his eyes. "Then I'll just have to return another day with a court order that will require you to sign."

He would do exactly that, I had no doubt. Although I had never heard of an estate being probated which belonged to an absentee body, I knew enough about the laws of probate and inheritance to know that this man was likely following the correct procedure.

Mom rubbed her forehead as if she was massaging away an ache, and I spoke sharply to Mr. Rowley. "We understand that Mr. Ventris lived in a small house in the country and drove an old truck. He owned ten acres by the river. None of that is worth much."

I watched Rowley's expression as I spoke and found out what I wanted to know. He squinted at something above my head, cleared his throat, and rubbed the bridge of his nose. A lie was coming.

"Actually," he said, "my client knows that Ben Ventris's estate isn't valuable monetarily. It's just that he feels an obligation to undertake all the responsibilities associated with Mr. Ventris's earthly belongings, few though they may be. In fact, Mr. Ventris told my client some time before his death, that he intended to make a will and name my client as the beneficiary. So you understand, of course, that my client is simply wanting to carry out Mr. Ventris's wishes, as I'm sure you want to do also."

If we signed those documents, Rowley's client would be free to bulldoze his way through probate court. He would have no restraints in searching for any treasure that might be on Ben's farm. Rowley hadn't mentioned any western oil lands. Did he know about them? Were they important to his client?

Rowley pushed a little harder. "You are aware, of course, Mrs. Campbell, that your and your mother's statements about Mr. Ventis's body are already in official police records, so it's not as though you'd be admitting anything people don't already know."

My mother's chin jutted out, reminiscent of a bulldog's. "Well, then, why don't you just use those official police records?"

Ignoring her, Rowley turned to me. "What do you say? Shall I come back next week with a court order?"

"Oh, I don't think that will be necessary, Mr. Rowley," I said. "I'm sure you can understand our hesitancy about signing a legal document we know nothing about. Neither of us understands the law but we can work our way through this."

Mom looked shocked. She seemed about to speak, then pressed her lips together.

Smiling at Rowley, I opened the door. "Just put that affidavit you brought on the sofa as you are leaving. We want time to look it over."

Rowley tried to become friendlier, but it was obvious he had not had much practice. "Well, that's mighty fine, ladies." His good old boy demeanor was in high gear. "I'll just leave this with you and be on my way. It's a pleasure to get to know you ladies." He snapped the briefcase shut and stood.

"Mrs. Campbell, I've read several of your AP news stories and you've always done a fine job; mighty fine." His eyes narrowed. "Do you plan to return to your reporter's job soon?"

So, he was wondering how long I'd be a burr under his saddle. I wasn't about to tell him my plans, especially since I didn't have any.

"Actually, Mr. Rowley," I said, "I have a contract with a Dallas newspaper to write a bunch of feature stories and that's something I can do pretty much anywhere. I may be in Levi for several months or even longer."

Rowley nodded as he went out on the porch. Striding to his car, and opening the door, he bent over and flicked another speck of dirt from his shoe. My grandpa's criteria for sizing up a man was right on the money.

Locking the door behind him, I said, "I thought that ruse about giving us time to think things over was the best way to get him to leave. The gentlest way, anyhow."

My mother drew a shaky breath. "I'm going to have to file Ben's will for probate; I see that. There's nothing else to do. I don't want Ben's money nor his property. I don't think I have any right to it, but I sure can't let somebody else get his hands on it; Ben wouldn't want that."

"Who is this mysterious client that Rowley represents, anyway?" I asked, following my mother into the kitchen.

She measured coffee and water and soon had the coffee pot going. We sat down at the table to wait.

"Maybe Ben's killer is using another tactic to get at the gold. Maybe he's decided going through a lawyer is safer than adding another couple of murders to his list," I said.

"So you think Ben's killer is the same as the supposed heir? Could his client be Jim Clendon?" Mom asked. "I've never had a problem with Jim but you don't trust him, do you?"

"Only about as far as I could throw him, Mom."

"Maybe Ray Drake, or Hammer Ventris, or . . . who?"

"In thinking about possible candidates as a murderer, we have a pretty wide field to choose from: Ray Drake tops the list, actually. A Chicago hit man? He probably reads the papers and maybe he's heard a little bit about the possibility that Ben may have been rich. Yes, a hit man would think nothing of murdering a few more people."

The coffee pot was still so I went to the cabinet and pulled out two cups.

Mom shivered. "It still gives me chills to think Drake was sitting right here in my house."

Putting two napkins on the table, I set down our full cups. "He could be a tobacco chewer, too. However, that Red Man wrapper we found clearly points toward Jim. I'm sure his deputy's salary isn't that great. Maybe he has decided to go through a lawyer to try and become suddenly rich."

"Maybe the murderer is Rowley himself," Mom said quietly.

"Could be. Or, bad as you hate to think about it, Mom, Jasper may be involved some way."

Coffee sloshed from Mom's cup. "I can't believe you said that, Darcy. That boy is as honest as his mother, and Pat and I have been friends for a long time."

"Okay, Mom. Sorry I mentioned it."

She got up and went to the kitchen window. "That rose bush is so pretty this year," she said. "Ben always liked to putter around in his flowers. Darcy, I don't understand why any of this is happening. Ben didn't ever bother anybody. He was happy out there in his house by the river. I could see, though, that he had changed in the last few weeks, maybe about the time he went to New York City. He was worried that something was going to happen to him."

I got up to stand beside her. "Do you think he knew the person who was a threat to him?"

"Looking back, I believe he did. I wish he had told me or somebody else who he suspected."

"I wish he had kept you entirely out of the whole thing," I muttered. "If his handwritten will holds up in court, you are going to be a wealthy woman, whether you want to be or not, and more of a mark for a killer. And, if Rowley manages some sleight of hand, somebody else is going to get his hands on a lot of wealth."

"My head is splitting," Mom said. "If I am declared Ben's legal heir, it's going to make somebody awfully mad."

"Yes. I think we need some legal advice, Mom."

She nodded. "As soon as I take a couple of aspirins, I'm going to make an appointment with Jackson Conner."

I had not seen Mom's lawyer friend since my return to Levi. If anybody could give us direction on which way to go, it was Mr. Conner.

CHAPTER 18

At 9 o'clock the next morning, my mother and I were in the offices of Jackson Conner, a man who had been a lawyer in Levi longer than I could remember. Among his clients were numbered the school board, bank, and the biggest farmers and ranchers within a hundred miles. He drew up wills for every one of Levi's citizens who owned enough property or had enough children to need estate direction. I felt comfortable in talking to him. More importantly, my mother trusted him.

As soon as she had those aspirins yesterday, Mom phoned Mr. Conner. Then, she and I had a long discussion about what might happen if Ben's handwritten will became public knowledge. My, oh my, how tongues would wag! I could hear the gossips having a field day: "Did you know that Flora Tucker got all of Ben Ventris's money and land? That looks to me like they were a little closer than just friends."

This future gossip was another thing for which I could thank Ben. I was beginning to think that I liked Ben Ventris a whole lot better before I knew about that gold.

More deadly than malicious gossip was the trouble the will would stir up for us from those who wanted Ben's gold. Somebody had committed murder, not once, but three times, to be rid of anyone who stood between him and a fortune. Perhaps he thought he had pretty much cleared the field. After our local newspaper printed the notice of Ben's will, I could only imagine the rage that would fill the heart of that unknown killer.

First, though, we would need to determine whether a court would conclude that Ben's will, handwritten on a sheet of notebook paper, was valid. My mother assured me that anybody would recognize Ben's strong, backward-slanted writing. It was certainly distinctive but I doubted that Ben had written many letters. My mother could not be the one to verify that his will and signature were authentic, since she was the person who would gain from it.

How did one go about the process of validating a handwritten will? Were other samples of Ben's handwriting available? Most wills were certified by two witnesses. This will had no witness at all, so did that make it invalid?

Looking around at the walls of Jackson Conner's office, I saw that it was truly a man's room. Cedar paneling, two brown leather sofas, and a large chair were evidence of the owner's taste. Photographs of local scenes hung on the walls: two deer among a stand of winter-bare trees, someone in hip boots (Mr. Conner, perhaps) standing in the river with a rod and reel in his hands, a lovely picture of a plain, white church with a bell at the top and several people going into its wide open doors. I had seen that little church many times on my way to Granny Grace's land.

A pretty receptionist sat behind an oak desk in this outer room. As we were about to sit down, Jackson Conner opened the door to his office. The aroma of cherry-flavored pipe tobacco wafted out. I always associated that scent with this big, attractive man.

Holding wide his door, Mr. Conner smiled and boomed, "Come in, come in. Two of my favorite ladies. Have a seat, please."

Mom and I sat facing the lawyer's desk, in leather chairs similar to those in the outer office. Conner's swivel chair creaked as he returned to it.

"I haven't seen you in a month of Sundays, Flora. And Darcy, it has been a long time since we've talked. I heard you moved back to Levi. Mighty sorry about your husband."

Swallowing a lump in my throat, I smiled and said, "Thanks. I'm back home for a while, at least, maybe a long time."

"Do you ladies mind if I smoke?"

We said, "No" at the same time. In fact, I would have been disappointed if he had put away his pipe. For some reason, that cherry scent was relaxing.

Jackson Conner rearranged some papers on his desk and got his pipe going to his satisfaction. Next, he gave us his full attention.

"Now, ladies, what can I do for the two of you?" he asked.

As a young man, he must have been quite handsome, and now, with his white hair and handlebar mustache, he was not only attractive but distinguished-looking too. He flashed a roguish grin.

"You didn't hang out in a bar last night and get yourselves arrested on the way home, did you?"

My mother snorted. "You know better than that, Jackson Conner. No, our problem is not what we *have* done but rather, what we *should* do. And, I don't know if you can solve it or if anybody can, for that matter."

Mr. Conner's white bushy eyebrows rose. "It may not be as bad as you think," he said.

For the first time, I noticed the plaque on the wall behind him: "*If God brought you to it, He will take you through it.*"

"I've cleared my schedule for the next couple of hours, Flora. They are all yours, if you need them. I'm prepared to listen to whatever is disturbing you," he said.

Mom sat twisting the straps of her handbag for several seconds, then she blurted out the question that had kept her awake most of the night. "Why does all that stuff about a will being probated have to be published in the paper?"

Mr. Conner's eyes registered surprise. He knocked a fragrant chunk of charcoal from his pipe, cleared his throat, and said, "It's the law, Flora." Reaching into the glass canister on his desk, he pulled out fresh tobacco and began tamping it into his pipe.

"If you're talking about your will," he said, putting a match to the pipe's bowl, "it probably won't be necessary to run it through probate since practically all your property is in your and Darcy's names, jointly."

Mom was about to twist her purse straps off. "But what if there's no close family and the—what do you call it—the major heir in the will isn't even related to the person who died?"

"It doesn't really matter if the heir is related to the deceased or not. If the will is prepared correctly, nobody should object to its being made public. There's a good reason for the law being written that way. For instance, suppose a person dies after borrowing money from a relative and hasn't paid it back. In that case, filing a notice of probate alerts the person who made the loan. He could then appear before the court and present the signed document and be re-paid by the deceased's estate."

Mr. Conner paused, glanced at Mom, and realized he hadn't yet quite answered the question she hadn't quite asked.

"Also, Flora, it's just to let all the relatives and other possible heirs know about the probate of the estate. There could be a person who thinks he should have been given something but wasn't mentioned in the will. In that case, he or she might decide to file a claim against the estate."

Mom leaned forward. "Do you mean that sometimes a person who isn't mentioned in a will can file a claim and collect?"

Jackson thoughtfully replaced the lid on the tobacco canister. "Only if that person you're talking about has a legitimate document that proves the deceased owes him some money. Or if that person can otherwise prove he had a vested interest in the estate. Is there some reason you wouldn't want your will made public, Flora?"

Mom shook her head. "We're not talking about my will, Jackson. It's just sort of a theoretical question."

"I see." The lawyer blew a perfect smoke ring toward the ceiling.

I had some questions of my own. "Is it always necessary to have two witnesses to a will to prove that it really belongs to the person who signs it?"

Mr. Conner shifted his attention to me. "Not necessarily. That's the usual way it's done but there are other ways of verifying that a will was actually written by the deceased. Are we talking about a problem with your husband's estate, Darcy? If that's the case, I might need to do a little research since Texas law may vary some from Oklahoma law."

Shaking my head, I said, "No. It's not my husband's estate that is in question. It's just —"

He raised his hand. "I know. I know. It's just sort of a theoretical question. Now, ladies, let me ask you a sort of theoretical question."

Mom and I waited.

"Are the two of you actually undercover investigators from the state bar, here to determine whether I still know all I need to know about wills and estates and probate? Or are you asking these theoretical questions just in case you might need to know the answers in the future? Or, far more likely it seems to me, is there a problem that involves a will and you're a little reluctant to tell me about it?"

Mom and I looked at each other. I could see that we were going to have to tell this lawyer everything if we proceeded with the probate. Starting with just the bare facts might be a good idea.

Taking a deep breath, I faced Jackson Conner. "I guess one of the things we really want to know, and this isn't just theoretical, is this: suppose there is a handwritten will that's proved valid and it gives all the deceased's property to a person who isn't a relative. Suppose there's somebody else who isn't mentioned in the will but is trying to file a claim. This last person is doing his best to establish himself as the sole heir and executor of the estate. In that case, which person has the sounder claim?"

I tried not to feel like a child who has just asked her teacher a silly question as Mr. Conner scrutinized me silently for a few seconds. His reply was to the point and probably straight from a law book.

"A valid will always takes precedence over anything else except in the case of property that's owned jointly with the right of survivorship."

Drawing a deep breath, I relaxed. "That's what I thought, but it's good to hear it from an authority. Here are the facts, Mr. Conner: my mother is the sole heir under a will that is not quite the usual textbook case. In fact, she didn't even know about it until the person who made the will died."

Jackson Conner nodded, probably thinking he had it all figured out at last.

Glancing at Mom, I said, "Then we discovered there is someone who claims there isn't any will and he should inherit everything because—um—he was assured of this."

I now had Conner's full attention. He took the pipe out of his mouth, put it into the ashtray, and asked, "Is there a large amount of money involved?"

Carefully choosing my words, I said, "There may be, but as yet we don't know the amount or value of all the assets."

Mom frowned. "First of all," she said, "I don't care a flip about the money I might get if we probate the will. There are people who need it more than I do. In fact, I'm not sure who it rightfully belongs to."

Mom had never chased after the mighty dollar. She owned a beautiful old house now only because my father had seen it and the surrounding land as a good investment, many years ago. My parents had never done much to the house except paint it and update the kitchen. Mom had an income that allowed her to live well enough to suit her. Once again, this was due to my father's foresight in purchasing a life insurance policy through his job. In fact, it was my father's example that persuaded Jake to buy a similar policy.

Conner nodded. "Indeed. I know you've never been interested in money, Flora. That's one of the many things I've always admired about you, but sometimes the deceased wants a certain heir to have control of his property because he knows that person will follow his intent exactly. It's actually quite a large responsibility, the inheritance of wealth."

The lawyer's shrewd blue eyes narrowed. "We're talking about one Mr. Ben Ventris and his will, aren't we?"

She nodded toward me. "You lay it out for him, Darcy. You can do it a lot better than I can. Tell him about the visitor we had yesterday."

So, I did. I began with finding Ben's body in the cemetery, its subsequent disappearance, the death of the Oklahoma City antiques dealer, Ben's daughter's death, and the arrival of Ben's letter containing his handwritten will several weeks after his death. I finish by recounting that unforgettable visit from the lawyer representing an unknown heir who had not actually threatened us, but certainly implied that things would be better if we went along with his proposal. I placed the affidavit that J. Smith Rowley left with us on Mr. Conner's desk.

Jackson Conner grew very still as he scanned this document. When he looked at us, the twinkle was entirely gone from his eyes. "I know J. Smith Rowley," he said. "What a disgrace to the bar."

As soon as Mr. Conner said this, a bell rang in my memory. Rowley had looked familiar and I realized I knew him too. That is, I knew of him. He had gotten a lot of publicity a couple of years earlier when he defended three people who bilked a big Oklahoma City corporation out of millions. No wonder he could afford Gucci loafers.

Mr. Conner forgot to draw on his pipe. "I know Rowley better than I'd like to know him," he said. "Among the state bar, he's best known for his representation of a big-time drug cartel." He shook his head. "I'm sorry you two had any contact with him."

Mom made a "tsking" sound. "So you don't believe I'd have any trouble probating Ben's handwritten will even though I'm not related to him?"

"No, I don't. I feel certain any judge in the state would rule that will is valid, especially after I submit an affidavit saying I know the handwriting is Ben's. Did you bring the will with you?"

Mom drew the envelope with the will in it out of her purse and handed it to Conner. The map was folded on the inside of the will.

Conner's bushy brows v'd down over his nose. I could almost see the circuits connecting in his mind.

Looking up at us again, he said, "Before we go any further, I need to tell you something. Ben called me the week before he was killed. He wanted to come into the office to talk to me. He said he needed to have a will made. I believe his words were, 'I've got a bad feeling.'

But I was leaving town the next day for a long trial in federal court. I told him I'd get back to him the first thing on the following Monday. I remember that I reminded him that I was aware he owned a lot of land and making a will was the wise thing to do. He said a strange thing. 'It's not the land he's after, it's the gold. But he'll have some trouble finding it.' Of course, by Monday, Ben was dead."

Jackson Conner sighed and gazed out of his window. "I wish I had asked him what he meant but I didn't. And you told me that Ben believed somebody was trying to kill him, Flora?"

"I don't know if he thought somebody was trying to kill him," Mom said slowly. "He told me he had a feeling that something was going to happen to him."

Conner smoothed the will on his desk. "This is most certainly valid."

"But how can we prove that is Ben's handwriting?" I asked.

Conner rose and went to a cabinet behind his desk, returning with a manila folder. "I can prove that right here. I represented Ben's interests when he bought that western property a long time ago. I've got several examples of his handwriting on these documents. I can prepare an affidavit certifying that this is the handwriting of Mr. Ben Ventris."

Perching on the edge of his desk, Jackson held the papers so we could see the similarity in the writing with Ben's name on them. "Proving the will is no problem at all," he said, "however, we do have a problem and it is a real whopper."

He handed the map back to Mom. With Ben's will in one hand and the folder in the other, he walked toward the outer office. "Let me get my secretary started on this so we can file it today. It may be important to act quickly."

Returning to his chair, he settled back and regarded us gravely. "You may both be in immediate danger. If somebody wanted Ben's assets enough to eliminate everyone who might lay claim to them, that person is sure enough not going to stop now."

I felt frozen in my chair. My mother and I talking about danger was one thing; hearing this man, well versed in law and human behavior, voice our fear was quite another.

"There's another little wrinkle here that neither of you may have realized," he continued. "If someone is trying to file a notice of probate through J. Smith Rowley, they're going to be watching the courthouse and the newspaper very closely to see if anybody jumps in ahead of them. The news of this probate is going to leak out even before the notice hits the newspaper tomorrow."

My lips felt stiff as I said, "So, no matter what we do, we're going to be in danger."

"Yes, unless you do as Rowley wants, and give everything over to this anonymous person. I guess that would let you off the hook."

"I can't do that," Mom whispered.

"Then, let me warn you that you will be in danger even before the paper comes out in the morning. I'm quite sure that Rowley has someone watching the courthouse to see what is being filed. Can you two change residences for a while? I have an unused guest room in my house. I'd be honored if you'd come and stay with me until this settles down."

Mom smiled. "Thanks, Jackson. That's kind of you, but we'll be okay. We have an electric alarm system and Grant has someone patrolling our road."

Jackson Conner shook his head. "You need a whole lot more than a patrol, Flora. You're dealing with a person who has evil intent. You're going to need at least two full time guardian angels."

CHAPTER 19

Walking out of Jackson Conner's office, I silently mulled over what he had told us. The information was solid and direct, but it didn't leave me feeling any safer. Sliding into the driver's seat of my Passport, I snapped the seatbelt in place. Mom climbed in beside me.

"Are you cold?" I asked as she shivered.

Shaking her head, she said, "How under the sun did we get to be in such a predicament? I didn't ever want to be Ben's heir. Wills and things—they are for families, not friends."

"With all my heart, I wish that Ben hadn't been killed and we were not in this pickle. But, I guess if wishes were horses, beggars would ride," I said.

"It's all about greed, Darcy. The Bible warns against it, all the way through. Greed, resentment, a heart that gets taken over by hatred. And selfishness—not thinking of anybody else. Remember that the Lord Himself was betrayed by a person who loved thirty pieces of silver more than he loved his Friend."

Turning on the ignition, I put the car in gear. "What do you think about going to see Pat Harris? If she could just convince Jasper to tell Grant what he did with Ben's body, it might be a step toward solving this thing."

"Let's go," Mom said. "Pat lives out on Old String Road. You go past the courthouse then turn right and it's about five miles out of town."

"Old String Road?" I said. "I don't even want to ask how it got its name."

Mom smiled. "It was a long time ago. An old man lived out there on that road in a little shack, all alone, for years and years. He'd pick up every piece of string or scrap of paper he found, smooth it out, and take it home with him. He was a hoarder. People started calling him Old String and forgot all about his real name. When he died, the story was that his house was crammed full of junk with only a little pathway to get through."

It takes all kinds of people to make a world and Levi seemed to have more than its share of the colorful kind. Slowing down as we passed the courthouse, I pointed to a figure in a long-sleeved shirt going up the steps.

"Look at that man. Isn't that Jim Clendon?" I asked.

Mom gazed out the window. "I believe it is. I wonder what he's doing."

"Maybe he's just going to Grant's office," I suggested, "or maybe he's keeping an eye on who files affidavits."

"Yes, there's that tobacco wrapper that certainly looks suspicious but, Darcy, we can't suspect everybody."

"Why not? A treasure worth millions would be a pretty good reason for some people to commit murder. As you said, Mom, greed is at the root of lots of the world's troubles."

"Jim Clendon is not likeable, Darcy, I'll agree," Mom said. "Maybe something happened to sour him on the world and maybe he suspects us just as much as you suspect him."

Maybe. But first impressions are sometimes correct impressions and my first impression of Clendon was not one to inspire confidence.

Mom pointed to a road sign. "Turn here."

Sure enough, "Old String Road" was emblazoned on the sign. Funny that I didn't remember this road.

Squinting up at the sky, I said, "Clouds are building in the west. Could be we're in for another storm."

"My bones are agreeing with you. My right big toe has hurt all day. See that little falling-down shack way back among those trees? That was Old String's place."

I glimpsed a sagging roof held up by weathered boards.

"Slow down, Darcy. That's Pat's driveway up ahead," Mom warned.

That was good advice. The bumpy dirt road was wide enough for only one vehicle and it was blessed with many curves that I couldn't see around. Trees pressed in from both sides. Around one final curve, a small, white frame house appeared. Red hedge roses bordered a gravel pathway leading to the front door. Stopping the Passport and turning off the ignition, I asked, "Do you think she's home? Things look awfully closed up to me."

"Let find out," Mom said. She slid out of the car and started toward the house. I was right behind her.

A large, red hound rose from a braided rug on the front porch. He came toward us, voicing his welcome with each step.

"Murphy! It's good to see you, boy." Mom bent to pat the old dog's silky head.

"Ben's?" I asked.

She nodded. "Pat said Jasper brought him home. He seems to have settled right in."

I raised my hand to knock and saw the curtain over the front window move. Pat's face peered out at us. I heard footsteps inside the house, a lock rattled, and Pat swung wide the door. "Flora and Darcy! What brings you here? Come in!"

Pat's living room was small and neat. Crisp, white curtains crisscrossed the only window in the room. A worn, gray sofa was against one wall. Two big over-stuffed chairs in a pink and rose print faced the sofa. A rocker, a short bookcase filled with books, and a small table with a television atop it completed the room's furnishings. I gazed at Pat's wood floor and admired the way it gleamed. Only constant care could keep the boards looking so good.

"Would you like a glass of iced tea? I just made some this morning. Sit down, if you can find a spot. I've been tatting and I got things in a mess," said our hostess.

Pat's definition of "mess" was not the same as mine. A blue wickerwork basket sat on the floor beside her rocker. A tatting shuttle and some intricate lace spilled out of it.

As Mom and I sat on the sofa, Pat vanished into the kitchen to get the tea. I leaned toward my mother. "How are we going to bring up the subject of Jasper?" I whispered.

Mom smiled and said, "Let me do that."

Pat returned from the kitchen with a tray bearing three glasses, moisture beading the sides.

"Iced tea, the summertime drink of the South," Mom said.

In one sentence, Pat bridged the gap of diplomacy. Sitting down, she said, "I imagine you've come to talk about Jasper."

Nodding, Mom said, "Well, yes, Pat, as a matter of fact, we have. Do you know where he is?"

A shadow crossed Pat's face and she seemed to find something interesting in her tea. "No, Flora, at the moment, I don't know where that boy is. He's somewhere out in the woods. He likes to ramble around, keeping an eye on things, he calls it."

Ice clinked gently as Mom swirled her drink. "He paid us a visit the other night."

Pat looked up. "He did?

"Yes. He told us that he was the one who moved Ben's body, but he refused to tell us where he put Ben."

Pat scrunched shut her eyes for a second. Worry lines etched her forehead. "He told me the same thing. I don't know where he hid Ben. No more than you do."

Cradling my cool glass in my hot hands, I asked, "Are you sure, Pat? Can't you guess where he might have taken Ben? Did he bury Ben on your place?"

Sighing, Pat said, "No. No, I'm positive he didn't do that."

I sipped my cold, sweet, and refreshing tea. "Pat, if he would just talk to Grant, tell him that he found Ben and moved him, that would be at least one mystery solved in this awful riddle."

"He would never do that, Darcy. I know my boy and he's real suspicious of the law. In fact, he mistrusts most everyone but me and, I guess, you, Flora. You were his Sunday school teacher and you never let the other kids pick on him."

"Of course I didn't," Mom said. "Even children can be cruel. Sometimes it's on purpose and then again, they might not know any better. Grown-ups can be cruel too, but they don't have ignorance as an excuse."

"My Jasper." Pat shook her head. "After his dad left us, it was just Jasper and me against the world, seemed like. He was never good in his books; he'd rather be out in the woods. I swear he could talk to the animals. He found a baby owl once that had been injured and he took care of that bird until it was grown. It's funny—he's really good with electronics. If anything goes wrong with the television, he's as handy as the pockets on a shirt. Now, how can he know so much about that and not care about reading or writing?"

"The Lord gives everybody a gift," Mom said. "Sometimes it makes up for something else. We are all lacking in some things and good in others. Computers, for instance. If something goes wrong with Darcy's computer, she usually knows how to fix it, but I don't know how and don't care to learn. That's just people for you."

"But you're a good cook," Pat said, "and you've got to admit, Flora Tucker, that you have a green thumb."

This conversation was veering off our purpose. "Does Jasper ever come home?" I asked. "Surely he comes for food?"

"Yes, he comes and goes. He wouldn't leave me unprotected. He feels like his job is taking care of me, so even when I don't know where he is exactly, I figure he's around somewhere close."

What a strange young man. And busy! He was the self-appointed protector for us as well as Pat, but she seemed to accept the fact that her son was different. Did she also accept the fact that he might have killed Ben?

In spite of the tea, I felt overcome with weariness. Pat, struggling to raise her child alone, Jasper, being ridiculed by his peers; Ben, Skye, Jason Allred, all dead. And why? What made people blind to what was really important in the world? Why couldn't we all just accept each other and get along? That was the eternal question: why?

Setting my glass on the tray, I stood up. "Pat, when you see Jasper again, will you at least try to get him to talk to Grant?"

Pat arose too. "I'll try, Darcy, but I know he won't do it. You see, since he's the only one who knows where Ben's body is, he's afraid Grant will think he's the killer. He has a mortal fear of being locked up. I just don't think he would live if he couldn't get out in the woods."

Mom handed Pat her empty glass. "Thank you for the tea, Pat. Come see us soon. We don't get to visit often enough."

Walking to the door with us, Pat said, "I'll do that. You all come back too, and Darcy, I'll talk to Jasper, but I'm not promising anything."

Murphy rose from his rug and ambled to my car with us. I wondered if Pat would talk to Jasper about Ben's hiding place or if she would broach the subject of murder. As I climbed into my Passport, I had the feeling that all Pat's talk wouldn't do any good. Jasper wasn't about to let go of his secrets, any of them.

Driving back down the bumpy driveway much more slowly than I had driven in, frustration brought tears to my eyes. Our mission had failed. We hadn't accomplished anything.

"Pat's house is clean and cheery," I said. "Those roses are beautiful, so why do I have the feeling that it's a gloomy place? There seems to be a spirit of sadness hovering over it."

Mom gazed out at the trees, dappled by the sun. Another of those lovely blue-green birds streaked across in front of us. "I think it's Pat's fearfulness," she said. "Jasper is all she has and she is worried sick about him. If that boy were taken away from her and put in jail, she'd suffer as much as he would."

Maneuvering around a pothole, I said, "I just don't know what to do next, Mom."

"Wait and see what happens, I guess. Practice patience and be watchful and, most of all, pray a lot. Trust the Lord, Darcy. He will see us through."

I sincerely hoped Mom was right, but waiting was not easy. My inclination was to charge full speed ahead and get things done. Only thing was, now I didn't know in what direction to charge. Patience was a virtue I did not possess. I had a mental image of being in a room with a door locked from the outside. I couldn't get out and I didn't know what threat was going to come through that door next.

CHAPTER 20

Levi's weekly newspaper was delivered to my mother's front yard every Thursday by 7 a.m. If Jackson Conner was right, the danger we were in would be doubled when her notice of probate was filed.

Stepping onto the front porch with my cup of coffee, I breathed deeply of the peony and rose-scented morning. No paper yet lay in the yard, but then it was only 6:55. As I turned to go back into the house, I noticed a pickup truck parked on the road beside our driveway.

A cold twinge of unease caused me to pause. Who was that? Could Ray Drake have changed vehicles and still be stalking us?

As I stood on the porch, the door of the truck opened and a gray-haired man stepped out. "Good morning, Darcy!" he called. "Is everything all right with you this morning?"

Although I had not seen Chuck Sullivan for several years, I recognized him immediately. A few years ago, he retired from the Oklahoma City police force after being shot in the leg. I remembered hearing that he returned to Levi and moved into his parents' old home place outside of town.

Pushing open the front gate, Chuck limped toward me. He stuck out his hand. I liked his warm, firm grip.

"Good morning to you too, Chuck. What are you doing out our way so bright and early?"

"Grant is worried about you and your mom. He asked for volunteers to keep an eye on you two. There are three of us who take eight-hour shifts, just to make sure nobody is hanging around who shouldn't be."

So this was how Grant solved his deputy shortage problem. The rush of gratitude I felt toward Grant and these unselfish men warmed me.

"Thanks more than I can say, Chuck. You must have been out here all night. Come on in for a cup of Mom's coffee."

"Don't mind if I do. Miss Flora makes the best coffee in the whole state."

"I believe she has some fresh cinnamon rolls too," I told him. "You're welcome to both."

A familiar yellow Volkswagon Beetle slowed down as it reached the gate and Levi's morning paper sailed into the yard.

Trotting down the steps, I called, "I'll just pick up the paper, Chuck, and be right in."

Compared to big city papers, this hometown paper was thin. I flipped it open as I walked back toward the house, skimming through to the back page. There, in bold black print was the notice I had been expecting:

In the Probate Court of Ventris County, Oklahoma, in the Matter of the Estate of Benjamin W. Ventris, notice is hereby given that a petition to admit to probate a handwritten instrument to be the Last Will and Testament of Benjamin W. Ventris was filed in this court . . . .

Reading further, the clerk's signature was followed with Jackson Conner's name, address, and phone number. Mom's lawyer had worded the notice so that my mother was not mentioned but I knew that people would start guessing and the murderer would know for sure he wasn't the petitioner. He almost surely would have a pretty good idea of who it was that beat him to the punch.

Chuck Sullivan had been reading over my shoulder. Now, he followed me up the porch steps.

"You know, Darcy," Chuck said, "most folks around here believed old Ben was dirt-poor, but I always suspected otherwise. I investigated a case in Oklahoma City involving a murdered rancher. The dead man's land bordered some oil land that belonged to Ben and Skye. Since this showed up in my investigation, I knew that Ben had to have a pretty good wad of money to buy that chunk of real estate."

Both Chuck and I saw the package at the same time—a canister-shaped box wrapped in paper decorated with pink roses with a big bow on top. It was in the lee of the porch just behind a pot of Mom's red geraniums.

Before either of us could speak, Mom opened the front door. "Good morning, Chuck," she said, smiling. Stepping out of the house, she looked down and spied the package.

"Why, look at that!" she said. "Where did that come from? Did you bring it, Chuck?"

Chuck Sullivan shook his head. "Afraid not, Miss Flora. Wait a minute. Don't pick it up just yet. Let me take a look at it. I've been parked in front of your house all night and the only person I've seen anywhere close has been that newspaper boy a few minutes ago. Whoever put that package there must have come by foot. If it wasn't there yesterday, somebody was on the porch last night."

Bending closer to squint at the attached tag, Mom said, "It's got my name on it."

Chuck motioned us back. "Move away from it, Miss Flora. You too, Darcy. I want to check this out."

Chuck carefully picked up the package and turned it around, frowning as he did so. "It's not very heavy. Can't weigh more than three or four pounds. Were you expecting something, Miss Flora?"

My mother shook her head. "No. The only thing I can think of is a couple of weeks ago, I worked two days at the church rummage sale for Emily when she got sick. She said she was going to send me some flowers or candy. I'll bet that's what it is."

Chuck lifted the canister above his head to examine its underside. That's when I saw a tiny spot on the bottom that the wrapping paper had not completely covered. An inch of fine copper wire protruded. Realization hit me like a freight train as I remembered a case I had covered for my newspaper a few years ago. If this thing had a timer that had been activated by the movement of picking it up, we all might have only a few seconds to live.

Grabbing the package from Chuck's hands, I ran down the steps and flung it toward our neighbor's pasture. It tumbled end over end and lodged against the trunk of an elm.

"What . . ." began Sullivan.

All three of us heard it—a small pop like the breaking of a balloon. Mesmerized, we stared at a cloud of yellow dust pouring out of the box top. The dust cloud lasted for thirty seconds, then disappeared.

My heart hammered against my ribs and I turned toward my mother. She stood like a marble statue, staring at the pasture.

Chuck started down the steps.

"No! Wait, Chuck!" I yelled. "Don't go near that thing!"

He kept walking. "I'm not going anywhere close, Darcy. I'm going to my truck for my cell phone. Grant has got to get out here. If it's what I think it is, we'd all be dead right about now if you hadn't thrown that thing when you did."

Mom's eyes were big and scared. She tugged at my sleeve. "What under the sun are you two talking about? What was in that package?"

Putting my arm around her shoulders, I said, "I'm afraid it's poison dust, Mom. I wouldn't have guessed, but my newspaper covered a case like this a few years ago when a similar package was sent to the mailbox of a state senator. According to what we found out then, that yellow dust was made from a deadly plant that grows only some place in Africa."

Chuck climbed back up the porch steps, his cell phone in his hand and joined the conversation. "I remember that too, Darcy. The Dallas cops determined the device was gang-related. Nobody found the bad guys, but the police report said that not many people knew about that particular poison. That timing mechanism was a devilish trick."

Mom was shivering as if she were in a blizzard. "How about the senator? Did he die?"

Chuck nodded. "Afraid so, Miss Flora. He was dead when his wife found him but by that time, the poison had mostly dissipated. Enough was left, though, for the crime lab to analyze it."

Leaning against the porch railing, I whispered, "It sounds as if we are dealing with a big-time criminal, a professional crook."

Mom wobbled to the porch swing and sank down into it.

My head was swimming. As if from a great distance, I heard Chuck talking to Grant. "We've got some pretty heavy stuff out here at Flora Tucker's place," he said. "Somebody left them a surprise package that nearly killed all of us. Yes, certainly, they are both all right." He paused for a moment, then said, "Right. Will do."

Within ten minutes, the sheriff's white truck roared down the road and skidded to a stop beside Chuck's vehicle.

Grant sprinted up the porch steps and grabbed my arms, his face pale. "Thank God you're safe, Darcy," he said hoarsely. "You too, Miss Flora."

Turning to Chuck, he said, "The crime lab boys will be here in a few minutes. Let's take a look around."

I noticed that deputy Jim Clendon did not make an appearance.

Mom and I went back into the house. I felt as weak and shaky as she looked. Grant and Chuck were professionals. They could do their job with no assistance from us; besides, I felt the need for a cup of coffee.

My mother and I were sitting at the kitchen table, warming our cold hands around our coffee cups when Grant came into the kitchen, thirty minutes later.

Pulling out a chair, he sat down facing us. "Miss Flora," he said, "you've got to promise me something."

Puzzled, Mom gazed at him. "What is it, Grant?"

"You both need to get out of town for a while. I don't know why you haven't left before now." His voice and face looked grim. "Darcy may not have enough sense to realize the danger, but you do! The men I had patrolling your house didn't catch this guy who left the booby trap, whoever he is. He seems to always be one step ahead of us, and I don't know what he's going to come up with next. So I'm ordering you to leave. Go to Florida or somewhere else far away. Take Darcy with you. And leave immediately before your enemy knows what you are up to."

My face felt hot. I could think of no retort. This blunt man certainly wasn't the boy I had a crush on so many years ago.

Mom answered for us. "Thank you, Grant, for your concern and patience. You're right. The good Lord expects us to use the common sense he gave us. We have been a worry to you and those kind men who have been keeping watch over us. Darcy and I will leave for a vacation somewhere. The fault is mine, though, not Darcy's. She wanted to leave some time ago but I've been the willful one. Just trying to prove a point, I guess."

CHAPTER 21

After Grant and his men left, Mom and I continued to sit at the kitchen table, talking about what had happened and wondering where we should go. Knowing that someone hated us enough to kill us felt like a cold knot in my stomach. I had never come up against that kind of deadly thinking.

We knew of no way to combat an unknown enemy who struck, then disappeared. The next attempt against our lives might be successful.

"There's a killer roaming these hills who is quite inventive about thinking of ways to commit murder," I said. "I've been wanting to visit Georgia since finding out about Dahlonega and the gold. I'm sure Georgia is beautiful this time of year. I vote for going there as soon as we can."

My mother nodded. "I've wanted to go for a long time too. We could drive to Bet's in Fayetteville tomorrow, stay overnight, then drive on from there."

"Still not wanting to fly, Mom?" I teased, knowing what her answer would be.

"Not unless absolutely necessary," she answered.

I should have confessed to Grant everything we knew about Ben and his will and Jasper. If he jailed us for obstruction, that might not be the worst thing in the world. At least, maybe we would be safe in jail. I also should tell him about our plans to leave and our destination, but my wounded pride was still smarting. After being the recipient of his sharp tongue, I had no desire to talk to him again, although common sense told me this would be the smart thing to do.

Gritting my teeth, I dialed the sheriff's office. He was not in, his receptionist Doris Elroy said. I dialed his home. He was not there either. Feeling vindicated, I decided that I'd try again tomorrow.

Thunder rumbled in some dark clouds approaching from the west. Mom's toe and those clouds probably meant we were in for a rain. Ordinarily, I welcomed a good spring storm, but not this time. Thunder was noisy and might mask the sounds of an intruder trying to get into the house. On the other hand, what normal person would purposely be out in an Oklahoma thunderstorm? The answer to that came on the heels of the question: we weren't dealing with a normal person. Murder was not an action that a sane person would take. This thought did nothing to reassure me.

The rain began an hour later. It continued throughout that long day, while we ate supper and packed, and it accompanied my mother and me up the stairs to our bedrooms. Usually, rain on the roof was like a lullaby, but that didn't hold true tonight. I strained my ears listening for a noise not related to the storm, and heard my mother tossing in her bed across the hall.

"Mom!" I called, "Do you want one of those sleeping pills from Dr. McCauley?"

"No, I don't," she answered. "If someone is going to murder me in my sleep, I want to know about it."

The logic in that statement escaped me.

With rain pounding over my head, wind rattling loose windows, and old boards creaking and popping to accommodate pressure changes, I got very little sleep but, somehow, Mom and I survived the night with no visitor.

At six the next morning, rain still sluiced from the sky. I hoped that Jasper was safe and dry at his mother's house.

The aroma of frying bacon wafted up the stairway as I pulled on my old blue housecoat. For a second, I didn't recognize the disheveled woman with flyaway hair and bloodshot eyes that stared back at me from the mirror. If she were to see me now, the New York receptionist would certainly think I needed her beautician.

"It'd be nice if the rain let up at least for our drive to Fayetteville," I grumbled as I stumbled into the kitchen.

To my surprise, my mother was as bright as a sunbeam. "Oh, I don't know," she said, smiling. "I like a good rain and I'm looking forward to going to Georgia. Our ancestors came from northern Georgia, Darcy. Have I told you that?"

"Seems I've heard you mention it," I mumbled around a mouth full of toast.

"Maybe we can do some family research while we're there," Mom said, pouring coffee. "Wouldn't it be nice to discover some long-lost cousins?"

"M-m-m," I answered.

"Hurry, now, Darcy. Shake a leg. I'll take care of the dishes while you go get ready."

I gulped down most of the bowl of oatmeal and headed for the stairs. At least one of us felt cheery this morning.

By the time I showered, tugged on blue jeans, a yellow t-shirt and matching long-sleeved top, I felt better. Lugging our suitcases downstairs, I found Mom waiting by the front door. She wore what she called her "city clothes"—a blue denim pantsuit with flowers embroidered on the lapel and hem of the jacket. Blinking, I looked twice. She was actually wearing makeup!

"I'll pull the car out of the garage and get as close to the porch as I can," I told my mother while fishing in my purse for keys to the Passport.

"I won't melt," Mom assured me.

She sang "Amazing Grace" as we drove east toward Fayetteville.

Laughing, I said, "If I had known a trip would do you this much good, I would have insisted we go a month earlier. As a matter of fact, I believe I did suggest it."

"I know," she said. "I don't understand why I'm so happy, unless it's because this nightmare may soon be over. We just need to get out of the way now so Grant won't have to worry about us, and let him find and arrest the perps."

Grinning, I said, "The 'perps,' Mom?"

"Didn't I say that right?" she asked. "I think it's short for perpetrators. Isn't that what they say on TV?"

A conversation with my mother is never dull.

As we crossed the Ventris River Bridge, rain came down harder. Switching my wiper speed to "fast," I made sure the headlights were on. Driving in rain was never fun and the oily surface of the highway could become slick when wet. I didn't want to hydroplane. However, to me, a dangerous road was much more preferable to the man-made threat that surrounded us in Levi.

We both lapsed into thoughtfulness. The regular slap-slap of the wipers had a lulling effect and the rain seemed to be a curtain, shutting us off from the rest of the world. The shower, however, was increasing to a downpour and I slowed even more.

Mom must have been concerned about road conditions too. "You know Deertrack Hill is coming up," she cautioned. "That hill is treacherous enough in good weather."

"My thoughts exactly," I answered.

"The highway department installed a heavy-duty guardrail a while back, but I don't want us to be the ones to test it. This is not the time to mention it, but you do remember that a few people have rolled off that hill, don't you?"

Evidently, her euphoria of the early morning was evaporating. Driving in rain did nothing to help my nerves either.

"Yes, Mom," I said. "In fact, according to newspaper files, five cars have rolled off that hill. Two people survived. Three did not."

She sighed. "Well, just drive carefully."

"The only way to be truly safe is to pull off the road and wait for this rain to let up," I said, "but I keep feeling that we need to hurry. Do you sense that too?"

My mother was twisting her hands together nervously. "As a matter of fact, I do," she said. "I wasn't going to say anything about it."

Once again, the only sounds were the rain and the wipers and the hum of tires on the pavement. Not even one motorist had passed or met us since leaving the city limits.

Lightning cut a jagged path across the sky in front of us. I strained to see through the torrent pelting the Passport. Even with the wipers turned to high, the rain obscured my vision.

When I noticed fuzzy headlights in my rearview mirror, I felt a sense of relief.

"I guess we aren't the only goofy people out for a drive today," I said.

Mom craned her neck to look behind us. "Misery loves company," she said. "That car must have pulled in from one of the side roads because I didn't notice anyone following us out of Levi. Maybe they are going to Fayetteville too."

"The driver must be surer of the road than I am," I said, noting the speed the car was traveling. "Seems to me he's driving too fast. He's coming up behind us pretty quickly."

A mile before reaching Deertrack Hill, those headlights moved up even closer. In the mirror, the car reminded me of a dark monster with glowing eyes. Lightning flashed and I got a better look. I gasped and Mom turned to look at me.

"What is it, Darcy?"

My throat felt dry. "That car following us, Mom; I can't see it well, but it is a big car like the Buick Ray Drake drove."

My mother shook her head. "Surely it isn't, Darcy. Maybe it just happens to resemble Drake's car. There are lots of Buicks on the road."

I decided to check him out. "I'm going to slow down and give him a chance to go around me."

When I let up on the accelerator, the other driver did the same. A cold finger of fear traced its way down my spine.

I increased my speed. Our follower increased his speed. Trying to keep my voice steady, I said. "My cell phone, Mom. Get it out of my purse and punch in 911."

Mom fumbled through my purse and flicked open the phone. She groaned. "Darcy, the battery is dead."

Gritting my teeth, I realized I had forgotten to plug it into the charger last night.

"It's all right," I assured her. "I'll look for a driveway and pull in."

My mother shook her head. "I don't think we'll find a driveway until we get down the hill."

With the next flash of lightning, I knew the car following us was not Drake's. The silhouette was different. It was more square-topped with darkened windows. It appeared black in the eerie light. Something else seemed odd about the car. The windows looked recessed. But why would a car have recessed windows unless it was an armored vehicle? It looked like pictures of limousines used to protect dignitaries and government officials. Were we being followed by an armor-plated, bulletproof sedan? If so, for goodness sake, why?

If the other car was not carrying an important personage, why was it so equipped? Who else would need such a vehicle? With a quiet certainty, a word popped into my mind: mobsters. The sophisticated explosive device yesterday, the three murders committed while leaving no clues to the murderer, this bulletproof car behind us, all pointed to one suspect—a member of the underworld. The only organized crime figure who had visited Levi lately, to my knowledge, was Ray Drake, alias Cub Mathers.

But why drive a car so heavily protected if the driver's enemies were two widows? My mother and I were not known to be dangerous, but that car would have been worthy of the likes of Al Capone. Whoever our pursuer was, he must be paranoid.

The headlights following us which at first had seemed friendly now seemed ominous and threatening.

Mom twisted around to look behind us again. "Oh, no, Darcy! It is coming too fast. It's going to hit us!"

The big car nudged my back bumper. Mom cried, "Oh, my Lord, help us!"

The Passport fishtailed across the highway and I wrestled with the steering wheel until I finally got back into the right lane. My face felt stiff and I tasted blood where I had bitten my lip. Gritting my teeth, I muttered, "I can't let him pass." Newspaper articles of people being forced off the road raced through my mind.

The pursuer's headlights grew larger in my rearview mirror. The car was coming at us again.

"Hang on!" I hissed and hit the accelerator. The Passport responded and we surged forward. A road sign cautioning that the speed limit was twenty-five miles per hour passed in a blur.

Behind us, our tormentor came so quickly that we seemed not to be moving at all. The car was going around me, despite my best efforts. But then, I saw that the driver had no intention of passing. He pulled into the lane beside me. Now even with us, nose to nose, the sedan was pacing me.

The heavy car edged ever closer to the center line. Its passenger door was perilously close to my driver's side door.

Scooting farther toward the ditch, I glanced at my mother. She was praying as she clutched the dashboard.

A bolt of lightning slivered the sky, hovering long enough to make trees beside the highway stand out for a split second like some eerie black and white photograph. In that instant, I saw inside the metal hulk beside us. The car contained not one man, but two.

Struggling to stay on the pavement, we careened around the first curve down Deertrack Hill. Tires screamed. The guardrail was only a few inches away and below that was the Ventris River.

The other driver closed the gap between his passenger door and my door. The first bump was a dull thud as he struck and we skidded. Then, he whammed us again. Sparks flew as metal struck metal and my Passport slid. We hit the guardrail with a rending sound.

My forehead connected with the rearview mirror and Mom gripped her door handle as if it were a lifeline.

Terror settled into a cold, hard knot of fury in the pit of my stomach. I would not continue in this crazy race that we could not win, but I would not be at the mercy of this evil being who was playing with us as if he were a cat and we were the cornered mice. We had one chance, a slim one. Praying that we would join the ranks of those who survived a tumble down Deertrack Hill, I determined that we would indeed go over; not sideways, but nose first.

"Hang on!" I yelled. Stomping the accelerator, I wrenched the steering wheel to the right. The Passport lurched up and over the guardrail. The last thing I heard was the sound of that reinforced rail snapping like a popsicle stick.

CHAPTER 22

Something wet dripped onto my face. Very annoying. Did Mom know her roof leaked? Dad would never have allowed such a thing. My bed must be under a hole in the roof. Strangely, someone, somewhere, was groaning. Pain twisted my mid-section. Slowly, I raised my heavy hands and felt the seat belt stretched tightly around my waist. Horror gripped me as memory returned. I was the person groaning and my head, as well as my stomach hurt. This nightmare was real and I was not waking up safe and secure in my childhood bedroom.

With a huge effort, I opened my eyes. As my blurry sight cleared, I saw that a large, leafy limb encircled the front of my Passport. Odd! Were we in a tree? And why was my seat belt biting into my stomach? Fumbling for the catch on the belt, my fingers felt cold and stiff. Where was that buckle?

I remembered the sound of the guardrail snapping and then darkness closed in. We must be at the foot of Deertrack Hill. We had survived! My heart turned over. At least, I survived, but where was my mother? Twisting around, I saw that she was not in the front seat nor the floorboard. Had she been thrown out? Was she dead? My heart beat so hard in my throat, it nearly choked me.

Moistening my lips, I croaked, "Mom? Where are you?"

From the back seat, a faint voice asked, "Darcy? Darcy, are we alive?"

Relief washed over me, leaving me limp. I would have laughed but my face hurt. Mom's hands touched the back of my head. "I landed back here," she said. "I'm sort of wedged in but I don't think any bones are broken."

"Thank God," I breathed. Tears slid down my face. "I'm going to try to unfasten my seat belt. This good little car protected us. It didn't roll. It stayed upright."

Mom's voice shook. "It wasn't the car that protected us; it was an angel."

Pushing and tugging at the belt, I finally had enough slack to unbuckle and shrug out of it. Why hadn't my air bag deployed? Did the drag from the thickets on the side of the hill slow us down enough to cushion our abrupt stop against a tree? My driver's side window was completely broken out, but that was a blessing because my door wouldn't open. This window would have to be our escape hatch.

Feeling for my mother's hand behind me, I asked, "Can you crawl to the front?"

"I think so," she said.

"Good. I'm going out of this window, then I'll reach back in and pull you through if you can push with your feet."

Three minutes later we stood on the ground beside my wrecked Passport. Rain dripped off the leaves of the giant oak which had stopped our downward slide. Wet, bleeding, and shaking, Mom and I hugged each other and tried to breathe normally.

My mother's face was scratched but she seemed to be all right. "Are you sure you are okay?" I asked.

"After surviving that, I don't think I'll ever be afraid of anything again," she said. "I must be a pretty tough cookie."

"And a pretty brave one," I said.

Mom touched my face. "Oh, Darcy, your poor head is bleeding."

Gingerly, I felt of my forehead. My hand came away red and sticky. "It's okay," I said. "It probably looks worse than it feels. Believe it or not, it doesn't hurt much."

Shaking her head, she drew a deep breath and said, "At least we got away from that rat in the other car. Why on earth would anybody want to run us off the road?"

"Why indeed, Mom? Why do you think?"

She sat down on a wet, gray rock. "It's the same person who killed Ben and Skye, isn't it? The same one who sent that poison gas trap yesterday?"

"It has to be. And it isn't one. It's two. I saw inside their car."

An alien sound broke the stillness. "Shhh," I whispered. "I hear something."

At first, all we heard was the drip-drip of rain, then through the woods came the unmistakable murmur of voices.

"Maybe somebody saw us go over the guardrail," Mom whispered. "Maybe they are coming to help."

"Or maybe they are the guys in that thug car. Quick, we've got to get out of here."

Any attempt to run would be futile. Neither of us was fit for a fifty-yard dash. Tugging at Mom's hand, I urged, "Let's see if we can find a hiding place, something to cover us."

We limped downhill as fast as we could, until a dense sumac thicket blocked our way. I held my finger to my lips and pointed to the bushy clump. Sinking down to my knees, I crawled in as far as I could among the stalks. Mom followed. I motioned for her to lie down and spread some dead leaves over her, trying not to think of the ticks, chiggers, and possibly snakes who might call this thicket their home. At the moment, natural dangers dimmed in the light of deadly humanity.

A man's voice came clearly to my ears. "I tell you, there's no use in tramping through these miserable woods looking for their bodies. Nobody could survive going down this hill at the speed they went over. Come on, let's go."

The crashing in the underbrush grew louder. From my hiding place, all I could see between sumac stalks were the feet of the approaching men. One wore scuffed brown boots; the other, black lace-ups. Afraid to move so I could see better, I tried to breathe silently.

A rough laugh and then a second voice asked, "What's the matter? No stomach for a little blood? Help me open this car door. We've got to make sure they're dead."

The door of the Passport creaked as the men wrenched it open. I heard a muffled exclamation. "Not here! Then, where —"

"They must have been thrown out somewhere. Like I said, they're dead. Come on, we're wasting time. We've got to get out of here before somebody stops to examine the broken guard rail and alerts the police."

My stomach clenched. That guttural voice sounded familiar. It sounded like Ray Drake! So, he hadn't been working alone but who was his partner? Jim Clendon? The second voice wasn't Jasper's—I was sure of that much.

"Stop whining! You're a big city boy and you're soft. Me? I was born in these hills, know them like I know my own face. I'm going to look around. Go on back if you want, but I'm going to make sure those two didn't survive." He laughed, not a pleasant sound. "I don't know how you're going to go far, though. I've got the car keys."

Holding my breath, I heard footsteps nearing our hiding place. Mom's hand on my arm shook. Trying not to blink, I saw through the thicket, rain-stained boots step ever closer. The owner of those boots must have bent over to shove aside some low-hanging branches. His hands were inches from my face. In his right hand, he held a big, black gun. On the third finger of his left hand, he wore a gold ring, a ring whose replica now resided in my mother's recipe box.

Feeling more than hearing my mother gasp, I knew that she saw the ring too. I prayed that she would not give away our hiding place.

At last, these two moved away. Standing, I helped my mother to her feet, half expecting her to collapse from fright.

However, another emotion gripped her.

"That rat!" she hissed. "He's wearing Ben's ring. He cut it off Ben's finger and now he's wearing it! That low-down, dirty . . . ."

Never had I seen my mother so furious. Through these past weeks, she had been sad, worried, frightened, and very stubborn, but now, I feared she was going to race after the killer and attack him with her bare hands.

Holding to her arm, I cautioned, "I agree with your description, but we've got to get out of here. I don't think we are able to climb back up the hill to the highway and if we try, we will probably run into those two. I don't know where we are, but going down will be easier than going up."

Leading the way, I broke through briers and pushed aside saplings. Never again would I fear that the birds and animals were losing their natural habitat. Nature's greenery was alive and well and most of it seemed to be growing on the lower slopes of Deertrack Hill. Tree limbs slapped our faces and thorns grabbed our hands and clothes as we slid, slipped, and fell through an entangling wilderness on our way down to the Ventris River.

Finally, the hill ended in a dry stream bed. Sinking down on a large limestone rock, I tried to stop panting and breathe normally. My mother lay down on a bed of moss under one of the cottonwood trees.

She groaned. "I've got to catch my breath."

I dabbed my bloody forehead with the hem of my shirt. "Same here. Looks like the rain is getting harder. The only good thing about that is it'll wash away our footprints."

My mother rubbed her scratched arms. "I don't think we can leave footprints in flint rock and that's what most of this is."

She sat up and put her finger to her lips. "Darcy! Listen! Do you hear that?"

I froze. Something moved through the trees above us. A deer ambled out of a thicket and I started breathing again.

"Whew! Scared me to death. Mom, do you have any idea where we are? Should we go right or left here? I'm guessing this was once a creek on its way to the river. I'm surprised there's not water in it after all the rain we've had."

She pushed a wet strand of hair from her eyes, stood up, and looked around. "Oh, I'm so upset, I can't think straight," she said.

"Hurry, Mom. Where would Ben's house be from here?"

She looked down at me, "Well now, Darcy, if I knew that, I'd know where we are, wouldn't I?"

With my head on my knees, I mumbled, "I'm sorry. We don't have any time to waste. Those two are probably still after us. If we could get to Ben's house, we'd be close to the road and civilization. And help!"

My mother grabbed a low-hanging limb for support and stretched up on her tiptoes. With her other hand, she shaded her eyes from the rain and peered into the woods.

"Let me think—I am pretty sure that our old home place and Ben's, across this creek, would be in that direction." She pointed to her right. "This little stream would be running into the one that divides our land, I think. It really looks different with no water in it. It must be dry because of the rancher who was damming the creek farther upstream. The law made him stop but he hasn't removed the dam."

Standing up from my rock, I gazed in the direction she pointed. In this weather, among identical trees, how could she be sure? One thing was certain: we couldn't stay where we were. Doubtless, those two men who ran us off the hill would not give up until they found us, and it didn't sound as if they'd hesitate to shoot us.

Looking down at my ragged outer shirt, I had an idea. Slipping out of it, I tore off a strip at the hem, then another.

"Darcy!" Mom's voice was sharp. "Have you lost your senses? What are you doing?"

"Creating a false trail," I muttered. "I saw Captain Kirk do this once to mislead some aliens."

With the strips in my hand, I ran in the opposite direction from which Mom had pointed. Hanging one strip on a wild rose bush, I trotted a little farther. Wiping that strip across my bloody forehead, I hung it on the low branch of a tree. Below the tree was a patch of mud. I pushed my shoe down in it, the toe pointing opposite our direction.

Mom actually smiled as I rejoined her. "Good job, Captain," she said.

"This ruse might fool them for a while, but not for long, I'm afraid. We've got to get going."

"Your poor head, Darcy. We need to put something around it. It's bleeding quite a bit."

"No time. Let's go."

"Let's stay in this dry creek bed," Mom said. "They won't find our trail quite so fast if we don't leave any more footprints."

This time, she led the way and I followed. Running was nearly impossible. Stumbling after my determined mother, I tried not to think about my throbbing head. When she stopped abruptly, I bumped into her.

"There!" she said, pointing to an overhanging bluff. "I know where we are now! That is the old river channel. It used to run right against that bluff before the dam went in and changed it. If we can climb that cliff, we can make it to the road. It should be about a mile farther that way, as the crow flies."

Lucky crows, not to have to bother with sharp rocks and limbs that reached out to grab us. Limping after my mother, I scrambled up a bushy rise toward the outcrop of gray rocks. I could see the old river channel, curving snugly around the bottom of the bluff.

Mom stared at the dry bed. "It always had water in it; now, it's as dry as a bone. Anyway, it's easier to cross now that it's dry. I hope that hill isn't as steep as it looks from here."

We hurried to the foot of the bluff and began to climb. "I'd prefer Mt. Everest to a bullet from that ugly-looking gun," I said between gritted teeth.

Finding an overhang on the bluff, we stopped to catch our breath, if only for a moment. The rock that jutted out gave us a brief respite from the rain but we'd soon have to leave its shelter. We couldn't rest long.

Something brushed past me and an eddy of wind fanned my face. I jumped and clapped my hand over my mouth to muffle my yell.

Mom caught her breath. "It was only an owl," she said. "We must have disturbed his resting place."

"Only an owl? What is it with these owls? I cannot believe they were once my favorite bird. Remember all those owls I've seen lately? Something always happens right after I see one."

I was babbling, I realized, and not making a lot of sense.

Mom patted my arm. "I know, but an owl is only a bird, not an omen. There have always been lots of owls in these woods. Oh, I wish I knew if we are actually close to Ben's farm and our own land. I think we are, but I can't be sure."

I gripped my mother's arm as a sudden thought struck me. "Remember what Emma said, Mom? She said that map of Ben's had the Cherokee word for owl on it. Do you think that owl might mean we are close to Ben's treasure?"

She shook her head. "Darcy, your hand is as hot as fire. You're burning up with fever."

"I'll be fine, but we've rested long enough. Come on, we've got to climb the rest of the way up this hill."

As we moved from under the protection of our limestone ledge, rain and wind battered us. The storm seemed to be in league with our pursuers, making our escape as difficult as possible. The only good thing was that those two men were battling the same storm. Of course, they didn't have to contend with a scalp wound and cuts and bruises.

Wind-driven rain rushed at us with such force that we could not see where we were going. Groping blinding from one rock to the next, I crawled over rotting logs and sharp rocks, Mom right behind me. I prayed that we would not disturb a cottonmouth or rattlesnake. Probably, our hands and knees were a bloody mess, but there was no time to worry about abrasions.

We must have been halfway up the bluff when I realized that I no longer was being rained on. "What—what is this?" I croaked.

My mother crawled up beside me. "It another ledge, Darcy. I think it's a small roof over an opening in this cliff. It looks like we've found another shelter."

"A shelter?" I stuck my arm into the indentation under the rock. "How far back does that hole go?"

Pushing matted tendrils of hair from her face, Mom squinted into the dark space. "I can't tell. Can't see very far with no flashlight."

"Unfortunately, the flashlight and our purses are probably strewn somewhere between the top and bottom of Deertrack Hill," I said.

Sinking to her knees, Mom sighed. "Oh, it feels so good just to get out of that rain and rest a minute. I'm bone tired."

"I know," I muttered. "So am I. We've got to keep going, though. If those two thugs catch up with us, they'll think nothing of adding us to their list of victims. Surely, we are almost at the top of this bluff. Maybe from there, we can see some familiar landmarks."

Taking the hem of her shirt, Mom dabbed at the blood trickling down my head. "This overhang juts out so far, Darcy, we're going to have to backtrack to find a way around it. We're kind of blocked from climbing up this way."

The thought of leaving our small protection and going back into the rain did not fill me with anticipation. Going down would only put us closer to those men stalking us. Waiting here, though, we would be like fish in a barrel, just hoping that Drake and his friend would not find us.

Mom's face began to look hazy and a strange blackness crept around the edge of my vision. Leaning back against the rock, I felt the pain in my forehead begin to engulf me.

As if from a great distance, Mom said, "Darcy! Don't pass out. Hang on."

Forcing my eyes open a slit, I saw her bending over me. Once again, she was wiping my face with her shirt. "Are you going to be all right?" she asked.

"I think so," I whispered. But, I felt cold and very, very weary. I had no strength left to continue and I had no idea what we should do next.

CHAPTER 23

Shaking her head, my mother said, "It's no wonder you felt faint, Darcy. You've lost quite a bit of blood. Maybe, just maybe, those men won't see us here. At least, we're out of the rain and wind. If we scrunch down as small as we can . . . ."

Drawing my knees up to my chest, I said, "It's a risk, but we may not have a choice. What if they were to come in this direction while we're out in plain sight, trying to find a way up the hill? It looks like we've painted ourselves into a corner."

Mom nodded. "I think we've about gone as far as we can go," she said.

Our trap was so efficient, it might have been designed by those diabolical killers who were chasing us. The rocky indentation where we sat was small and bottle-shaped, with the entrance being the neck of the bottle. It was no more than three feet high and four feet wide, barely room enough for two muddy, battered, and bloody women to crouch. Although it was tiny, cramped, musty, and dank, compared with what we had been through during this unbelievable day, it wasn't bad. The old saying, "Between a rock and a hard place" came to mind, an apt description of our predicament.

"Please, God," I whispered aloud, "don't let this tiny closet of Yours become our tomb."

Mom nodded. "I believe that God will get us out of this mess, Darcy. I don't think He has brought us through everything just so we could end our lives out here in the woods."

"If you believe that, I'll try very hard to believe too," I said. "Remember that plaque on Jackson Conner's wall?"

Together, we repeated, "If God brought you to it, He will take you through it."

Mom squeezed my hand.

I was freezing and my mother must have been just as miserable as I was. We were wet, tired, and, I realized, hungry. The time of day had no meaning. Was it still morning, or afternoon, or nearing night? This cloudy twilight had been with us since we left home this morning, and I felt like I had been running for a year. Already, my mother's warm kitchen seemed light years in the past.

Rubbing my stomach, I said, "What I wouldn't give for a cup of your hot, strong coffee."

"Same here," she answered.

The bone deep chill that caused my teeth to chatter seemed to come from inside. Perhaps this is how people felt when they were looking death in the face. True, we were in a physical trap but a snare had been tightening around us since we walked out of Jackson Conner's office. The killer, or killers, had likely been watching us then, a surveillance that continued through the night.

For a few seconds, I wondered why those men, the ones who had three murders to their credit, had not broken into my mother's house and attacked us while we slept, but then, I answered my own question. Yesterday we thought there was only one man after us. He must have decided he needed help and called in his buddy to finish the job. Who were they? Drake and Hammer? Drake and Clendon? Drake and an unknown person? Where had they gotten the heavy car that tried to force us off Deertrack Hill?

I voiced my thoughts aloud. "Those crooks planned to run us off the road and make it look like an accident. That's why they had an armored car; they wanted to be sure to get the job done. I wonder where they found such a vehicle. Not in Levi."

"Nobody would have questioned our deaths, Darcy. People would have said we were driving too fast on a rain-slick highway. That's why they didn't shoot us. They wanted our deaths to look like an accident," Mom said.

A new thought surfaced in my foggy mind. "It almost looks like two killers with different methods. The two men and Skye might have been killed by someone who was angry—enraged because they wouldn't tell him what he wanted to know. But, if our deaths were to look accidental, it would have taken some planning."

"And that poison bomb, Darcy," Mom said. "That took some knowledge of such things.

I bent forward, hugging my knees and trying to stop shaking. Why had Ben gotten us into this? Why was it so important to keep the hiding place of that gold a secret that he would risk my mother's life by making her its protector?

One way or another, the killers were determined to get that gold, and it didn't seem to make much difference which method they used. Did they really think my mother knew the location of the treasure? Did they want only the map? Was the map the reason those three people were killed? To my mind, that ancient map would not help anybody. The area had changed and the scribbled lines were dim, without any sort of recognizable landmark.

Turning my head to look at my mother, I asked, "If we offer those guys the map, do you think they'll leave us alone?"

Mom patted my shoulder. "I don't think so, Darcy."

We had played right into the hands of the killers by being out alone early this morning. Why had I forgotten to leave a message for Grant telling him where we were going? Why had I been so arrogant as to get involved in this brutal case in the first place? At least Aunt Bet knew we were coming. She would surely alert the authorities when we didn't show up. When Grant couldn't find our bodies in my wrecked Passport, he would search for us, wouldn't he?

Then I brought myself up short. Mom had insisted that nobody was going to drive her out of her home. She hadn't changed her mind until after that bomb. Perhaps, a niggling voice in my head insisted, this was meant to be. The owl that flew up was a warning to us. Maybe our deaths were imminent and we could no more have avoided this situation than we could have avoided the rain-filled clouds that were steadily darkening the entrance to our little rabbit hole.

A drop of blood dripped from my nose and I flicked it away. I felt terrible and could not imagine how I looked. If our lifeless bodies were found, would anybody recognize us?

"I'm in no condition to die," I told Mom. "Just look at my hair. If Minda Stilley could only see me now." I tried to grin but my teeth must have cut my mouth. It hurt.

Mom scooted closer to me. "Don't say that. I'm not wanting to go just yet."

The front of my yellow knit shirt was soaked with blood, mud, and rain, and my jeans wore red splotches.

My mother wasn't much better off than I was. The only difference was that she didn't have a head wound that kept bleeding. She had sliced her knee on a sharp rock, and her once-pretty denim pants were ragged and soggy. Although the day was warm enough, rain-cooled but still it was a spring ran, we both shivered as if a frigid January wind blew against us. I felt dizzy and disoriented and Mom probably felt the same; she just wasn't the complainer that I was.

"I wonder how long it'll take for them to find us?" I muttered. Maybe fifteen minutes of going in the wrong direction, if they fell for my trick of putting bloody strips to mark a false trail, and then circling around until they found evidence of our flight. We had kept to the rocky creek bed, but sooner or later, they'd find a hair, or a broken limb, or a spot of blood. I had no idea how long we had been running. It felt like forever.

Once again, Mom was the one with coherent thoughts. "We've got to find something to stop your head from bleeding," she said, looking around her.

"Good idea," I mumbled. "What do you have in mind?"

She leaned back, wriggled out of her canvas shoe, and began peeling off her knee-high hose. "It's not much," she admitted, "but maybe it'll help some. I should have done this a long time ago."

"We didn't have time to stop. But thanks, Mom."

At least the hose soaked up the blood, keeping it from dripping into my eyes.

I looked around us. "Since we are pretty much trapped here, could we camouflage the opening in some way?"

"Let's try," Mom said, crawling back to the little entrance. "There are some sticks and dead leaves on the ground out here."

I crawled out from under the ledge too, and grabbed some of the small limbs that had fallen off the trees last fall. The brown leaves should help to hide us. Scooting backward under the outcropping, we pulled the sticks and leaves in with us and arranged them across our little hole. Hopefully, nobody would get close enough to peer in.

On a sunny day, anyone could detect our hiding place but the clouds were in our favor. Our hope lay in trying to blend in with the terrain.

"I feel sure we are on Ben's land," Mom said as we dusted off our hands and resumed our cramped positions. "Once we are able to leave this little nook, it can't be too far to his house. Then, hallelujah, we can flag down a passing car, or at least find a better place to hide. We must be near that little hill behind Ben's barn."

Unfortunately for us, the threatening sky lightened at the same time I heard rocks rattling nearby. My blood seemed to turn to ice and my shaking resumed in full force. Rain would have helped to hide us. If the sun came out, our enemies could quite easily see where we crouched.

That familiar, guttural voice came closer, evidently displeased and grumbling. The second voice answered. From the snatches of conversation I could decipher, I gathered those two were displeased and arguing. Then the talking stopped and the sound of feet crunching through sticks and kicking loose rocks grew nearer.

Ray Drake's partner spoke. "I used to tramp all over these woods. We'll find those two if we have to check under every rock and behind every tree. They aren't getting away. That much, I can promise."

My heart thumping against my ribs, I scooted toward my mother. We put our arms around each other. If we were going to die, at least we would die together. Shrinking against the cold, hard wall of our prison, I felt the rock pressing into my back.

CHAPTER 24

Perhaps extreme terror sharpened my senses. Maybe desperation whispered that I shouldn't give up yet; whatever prompted me, with death snarling up the cliff toward us, I made a startling discovery. My mother and I had scuttled as far as we could go under the ledge. We were backed against the wall of this natural grotto and could go no farther. The wall of the cave pressed against the left side of my back, but there was no support behind my right side. Why was that? Was I feeling an uneven place in the rock or was there a hole behind our hiding place?

Twisting around, I managed to work one arm behind me into what seemed to be an offset in our enclosure. My fingers probed a fair-sized opening we had not noticed when we crawled under the ledge. Was it only a shallow cleft in the rock? Cautiously, I ran my hand along the smooth, dry sides of this area that I could not see, but only feel. Gently, I patted the floor of this space, and traced a square shape, like a step. Leaning farther backward, I felt another square below this one. My heart turned over. These were steps. How far down they went and where they led, I did not know nor care. They offered the possibility of a better hiding place and I did not question the serendipitous finding.

Shaking my mother's arm, I leaned close to her ear and whispered, "Don't say a word, Mom. Just follow me."

Flopping onto my stomach, I squeezed, head first, down the first two stone steps. I heard my mother slithering along behind me. The passage through which I slid was narrow with barely enough room for my body to pass through. Raising one hand over my head, I felt nothing but space. Cautiously, I rose to my knees, then to my feet. Unbelievably, I was able to stand. Stretching my hand as far as I could above me, I was not able to touch a ceiling. Although the height of this tunnel had increased considerably, it was barely wide enough to allow us passage. Slowly and carefully, I tested each step with my toe before moving downward. I inched along into silence as complete as a tomb except for the sound of my mother, breathing heavily behind me.

This was no labyrinth we traveled. No other tunnels intersected this one. The passageway led steeply down, with no twists and turns. With each step, we descended farther into the subterranean depths of Ventris County, and we were still as lost as we had been above ground.

I knew the moment our pursuers found our little hideaway. I heard that guttural voice exclaim, as if he were far away, "They aren't here!"

Grabbing my mother's wrist, we stood, hardly daring to breathe. Then, once again silence fell, as complete as the darkness that surrounded us.

Did we dare retrace out steps and crawl out? Was it safe or would Drake and his companion return?

Standing against the smooth walls of the tunnel for what seemed to be hours, I heard no further sound except the thundering of my heart and Mom's breathing.

Finally, she whispered in a voice that echoed eerily in that chamber, "Let's go on a little farther, Darcy. These stairs lead somewhere. Maybe there's another way out."

I couldn't argue with that, especially since I was too weak to face the possibility that if we returned the way we had come, we might crawl right into the arms of death.

Forcing myself to focus on each slow, sliding step, I fought the panic that threatened to raise its ugly head. Claustrophobia had never been a problem for me, but I could not see where I was going and the sides of this tunnel seemed to be closing in. I was definitely claustrophobic now.

Mom's hand pressed lightly on my back. I knew this was as much to comfort me as it was to be certain we were not lost from each other in the inky blackness. Would we suddenly step off into a bottomless pit and disappear forever? Silently, I prayed that God would guide us. What a time to remember stories of rattlesnake dens hidden far underground. My shivering shot into high gear.

I had always believed that I could choose my own thoughts. Unwelcome ones might come knocking, but I didn't have to invite them in. However, I had never before been below the earth in an unknown, unrelenting darkness with death waiting above and who knew what waiting below. Now, memories of teenage tales told at slumber parties or around a campfire crept up on me and I could not dispel them. Stories of unexplained lights flickering near old graveyards, of strangers who mysteriously disappeared, of eerie nighttime noises, not only knocked at my mind's door, they moved in and took up residence.

Sadly, I had not counted the steps as I descended. It was too late to do so now. Had we gone twenty or fifty feet under the earth? My head pounded and I labored to draw in each breath and expel it, fighting the urge to run back up to daylight and fresh air.

Mom saw it before I did. "Darcy," she whispered in my ear. "Look."

The blackness was no longer absolute. I blinked. Did I see a dim glow somewhere ahead? Rubbing my eyes, I looked again. Yes, there was no doubt about it. A faint light flickered below us.

Forgetting my discomfort, I hurried down the last two steps, which ended in a level stone floor. The flickering gleam came from a lantern hanging from a peg stuck into a crack in the cave wall.

Gripping my mother's hand, I pointed to that wonderful light, feeling like laughing and crying at the same time.

A lantern that was burning meant some human hand had struck a match to it and not so long ago that the kerosene had been consumed. A lowly lantern had never looked more welcome, no matter who had placed it there.

My mother breathed either an exclamation or a prayer that sounded like, "Dear Lord."

Closing my eyes, I wondered if I was dreaming but, no, when I looked again, the lantern was still there.

"Where are we, Mom?" I asked. "What is this place?"

"I have no idea," she said faintly. "I am just as dazed as you. Maybe we are both dreaming. Maybe that wreck injured us more than we thought. Maybe this is just an hallucination."

"I've never heard of a joint hallucination," I said, "but nothing is impossible."

Looking around slowly, I saw that we were in a circular area about the size of my mother's kitchen. The lantern dispelled total darkness, but it left much of the cave in shadows.

"I don't understand any of it," I said, "but I've never been so glad to see a light in all my life."

Where were we and who had been here before us? Who left the lamp and when did he light it? Would he return soon? Surely, that unknown person was not a threat to us. And, almost certainly, Drake and his friend did not know about this underground room or they would have been following us.

Mom's whisper seemed as loud as a shout. "A *kiva*," she said. "It must be a *kiva*. I've read about them."

"What are you talking about?" I asked, noting the way she was turning slowly around as she scrutinized the area.

"*Kivas* were places where early people would store their grain. Or, sometimes they were used as meeting places, or . . . I don't know, Darcy. It just seems to be a whole lot more than a cave."

I agreed. The flickering glow glinted on something on the wall near my outstretched hand. Stepping closer, I examined what seemed to be a drawing etched into the rock. Reaching up, I traced an outline of a figure.

It took a few moments for my vocal chords to work. Gulping, I said, "An owl, Mom. This is a drawing of an owl."

We both stared at the strange image. Curiously disproportioned, it had a huge, round body with a small head that was made up almost entirely of enormous eyes. Shiny, black pupils as bright as onyx glowed in those eyes. Had they been painted with some sort of glossy enamel? Were they circular pieces of a shiny, black gem? The murky light made it impossible to scrutinize them closely, but those eyes sent a chill down my spine. They seemed to follow me when I moved to the right or the left.

Turning to my mother, I sputtered, "The owl, Mom. Remember what Jasper said? Something about an owl knowing where Ben is. And then, that word on the map, the Cherokee word for owl."

Mom covered her nose with her hand. "That smell. I've just noticed it. Oh, Darcy! What is that horrible odor?"

Sniffing, I gagged. This was a stench that once a person smells it, they can never forget. I hadn't noticed it at first, but now a drought of air brought a repugnant foulness full force into my nostrils.

The sickening scent seemed to come from a shadowy object on the side of the cave farthest from the lantern. Pulling my t-shirt over my nose, I stepped closer. On the floor lay a bundle wrapped in what appeared to be a flowery, homemade quilt. The covering had slipped away from a green plaid shirt. One of the person's hands protruded from the quilt, a left hand with a missing third finger. We had stumbled onto the place where Jasper placed Ben. The quilt was undoubtedly one of Pat's. He had laid Ben where he would be safe, Jasper said, where Ben wanted to be.

My mother's raspy breathing was akin to gasps. "Is it . . . is it him?" she asked hoarsely. Then, she answered her own question. "It is. It's Ben."

At that moment, I would have given everything I owned to keep her from seeing this ghastly sight. But, of course, there was nothing I could do.

She swayed against me and I grabbed her before she slid to the floor. As I backed away from that awful bundle, I was unable to take my eyes off it. Now that we had found him, what could we do? Was Ben's tomb going to be ours too? Were two murderers waiting, even now, to shoot us if we dared climb up out of this cavern?

Drawing a shuddering breath, Mom whispered, "I'm all right. This is not really Ben. He has gone on to a far better place."

I tried to think of some sort of benediction I could give to Mom's old friend, but my mind was frozen.

"He was a good man," I said. "He is at peace now. He's with God."

In a rush, the events of this harrowing day caught up with me—the pounding in my head, the dizziness and loss of blood assaulted me in a wave of nausea. Fighting against the need to let go of consciousness and sink into oblivion, I struggled to remain on my feet.

Staggering a couple of steps, I leaned against the wall. At first, I thought the movement beneath my shoulder was just vertigo and I was losing the battle to stay upright. Was I keeling over like a root-pulled sapling, or had the wall actually moved?

I stepped away just as a portion of the side of the cave swung inward. A narrow panel in the solid rock moved backward as if on a pivot and disappeared while another panel swung outward, like a giant lazy Susan.

Rubbing my eyes, I blinked and looked again. Mom's quick intake of breath told me she saw the same thing. Unbelievable though it seemed, I had inadvertently opened a hidden compartment built into the side of this cavern.

The shock of this discovery kicked my flagging system into gear, and I stepped closer to this amazing discovery. Shelves lined the rock panel. Putting out my hand, I started to touch them, then drew back. On the exposed ledges within the panel lay two flat wood boxes and three leather drawstring bags. Both boxes had small lock plates made of polished metal that glowed a ghostly greenish yellow in the flickering light. I knew at once what those lock plates were made of and where the metal came from.

Mom whispered, "Could this be what Ben was murdered for? Is this his gold?"

Ben had told the New York City antiques dealer that the medallion had come from a trunkful of other gold objects. Did those boxes and bags on the shelves contain the rest of Ben's hidden treasure? People had searched, lied, and killed in attempts to find the hiding place and yet we had stumbled onto it accidentally. It must have been decreed somewhere that two bumbling, sick, and terrorized women were to be the ones to uncover an ancient mystery.

Finally, my curiosity overcame my amazement. "I've got to know, Mom," I said. "What is in those two boxes and those leather bags? Is it really the gold from Georgia? We've suffered a lot because of a hidden treasure and I've got to know if we've found it."

My mother nodded. Silently, she reached for the box nearest to us and lifted the lid. The lantern's light glinted on a treasure straight out of the dream about a pot of gold at the end of the rainbow. Neatly arranged in a tray, laid out carefully side by side on strips of something that may have been deerskin, lay the Dahlonega gold. The items ranged from a hair ornament the size of a rosebud to a medallion shaped like a flying eagle and as big as a silver dollar. Every priceless piece shone with the same strange luster that identified my mother's ring.

I counted four rows and a dozen items in each row. Mom replaced the lid on the first box and opened the second one. It too contained four neat rows of gold pieces whose exquisite workmanship spoke of expert goldsmiths. Each item was perfect in shape and balance. Carefully, I lifted out an intricate butterfly. Even the tiny antennae were lifelike. Dust from the leather bag had settled over its outspread wings. Gently, I rubbed it with my finger. Feeling as if I could gaze at this lovely object forever, I understood the greed that took over the lives of men and drove them to commit lawless acts. I understood what it meant to have gold fever. I placed the butterfly back into its bed.

Reaching for one of the pouches, I loosened the drawstring, and shook out its contents. Gold nuggets lay in my palm. These chunks of precious metal ranged from the size of a marble to a golf ball. Each bag was approximately six inches long and perhaps six inches around. Losing track of time, I stared until my mother shook my arm.

"Let's put it all back, Darcy," she said. "And we'll shove the wall back around so they are hidden again."

Air whooshed from my lungs. "Mom! Do you realize what you are saying? Do you want the gold to just stay here forever?"

"Think, Darcy," she said. "If we don't get out of this dungeon, all the gold in the world won't do us any good."

Replacing the bag, I pushed the edge of the rock lazy Susan. It obediently turned until it became part of the cave wall once more.

My legs trembled so badly, I could no longer stand. Sinking down on the cold floor, I gazed up at the owl etched in the wall beside the hidden door. In this one room were Ben, the owl, and the gold.

Shaking my head, I said, "I wonder if Jasper knows about the gold or if he just happened to find this cave and thought it was a good hiding place for Ben?"

Mom spoke softly. "I've been thinking about where we are, Darcy. I believe this cave might be right under Ben's pasture. I'm pretty sure we were on his land when we hid under that ledge that was the doorway to the cave."

"Maybe that ledge was the spot marked on the map. Do you think?"

She shrugged. "The area has changed a lot since the map was made—how long ago? A hundred years? Two hundred?"

"I don't see how Jasper could have carried Ben down that long flight of stairs. It's too narrow and that would be almost impossible, even for someone as big and husky as Jasper."

"Well, then," Mom said, "there must be another way of getting into this cavern."

With the gold out of sight once more, a measure of my clear thinking returned. "I'm going to look around this room and see if there's a door somewhere."

Unhooking the lantern from its peg, I held it above my head, and walked slowly around this circular cave, running my hand across the wall as I walked. Close beside Ben's body, I touched wood. Holding my lantern closer, I saw a doorknob protruding from an ordinary-looking door.

I shouted, "Mom! Come take a look at this!"

"What is it?" she asked, purposely averting her eyes from that pitiful bundle wrapped in the quilt.

"It's a door, but I think it's stuck. Help me pull."

I yanked on the door until it creaked open a couple of inches. My mother slid her fingers into this crack and pulled as I tugged on the knob again. With a nerve-shattering shriek, the door swung inward on rusty hinges.

The lantern shone on an earthen tunnel which slanted upward. I didn't care how steep it was, since the direction was up instead of down.

"Hurry! Hurry," I urged. "This has got to lead to the light of day and freedom! Come on, Mom."

She hesitated. "Darcy, wait now. We know that we can get out by going back the way we came. Maybe Drake and his friend are long gone by now. We don't know where this doorway leads. We could be walking into a trap."

Pausing, I thought this over. She was right, of course. On the other hand, the two crooks could still be looking for us in the bluff area. And, after we had retraced our steps, we still wouldn't know which way to go to get help.

"This can't be any more dangerous than finding ourselves on that bluff again, Mom. Remember, we were trying to find a way off it when we discovered that tunnel."

She looked at Ben, her eyes brimming with tears. "Jasper was right. Ben is where he would want to be. In a way, I guess he's buried. He shouldn't be moved. Maybe we ought not to tell anybody about finding him or the gold."

Now, I was worried about her mind. She wasn't thinking clearly. "You know that we'll have to tell Grant, Mom. He has to know everything, and this time, I'm not keeping anything a secret."

"I believe in respecting a person's last wishes," Mom said. "This would be what Ben wanted."

What I wanted was to scream. "Mom," I said as patiently as I could, "Ben is dead. He's dead! What he wanted doesn't matter anymore. And it is all Ben's fault that we are in this predicament, running for our lives.

Why on earth did he tell you anything about that gold? He sure wasn't thinking about your welfare."

"Darcy!" Mom looked as shocked as she sounded and I was immediately sorry for my outburst. "Ben didn't ask to be guardian for this gold, either."

"I know, I know. It was handed down to him by his father and grandfather. The point is, the secret could have died with him and I quite frankly wish it had."

"You'll feel better when you are safe," Mom said.

Gritting my teeth, I held my tongue. Grasping the lantern and my mother's hand, I squeezed through the door and started up yet another tunnel, this one made of dirt.

My legs ached as I leaned into the path that slanted sharply upward. Silently, I prayed that this dark passageway would not turn out to be our grave. My fondest hope was that I would not be buried until after I died.

CHAPTER 25

When it seemed as if I could not climb another step and my lungs were on fire, a current of cool air brushed my face. Mom felt it at the same time.

"Stop for a minute, Darcy. Let's rest. I can breathe better, all of a sudden. There's fresh air coming from somewhere."

The breeze moved my hair and relief flowed through me. "Wonderful!" I said. "Praise the Lord! We are heading toward an opening to the outside world."

Once again, I put one weary foot in front of the other, buoyed by the hope that our nightmare might be ending. I was about to stop for another breather when Mom said, "Up ahead! Look, Darcy! There's a light."

She was right. The dim light of day filtered into the darkness and my weariness vanished. When I was younger, I went spelunking with Jake, but if I got out of here, never again would I willingly set foot below the ground. Maybe I would just re-think my final arrangements and ask for my earthly resting place to be a mausoleum. Anything would be fine, as long as it was above the ground.

Abruptly, the tunnel came to a dead end with a wide board wall blocking our way. A sliver of light and a current of air pushed through a crack in the wall.

Gasping, I said, "I don't see a door. How do we get out of here?"

"Maybe we just pull," said my matter-of-fact mother. "Let's grab hold of these boards."

"Got it," I answered. "One, two, three, pull!"

We both tugged with all our strength. The heavy boards inched toward us.

"Once again, Mom." I panted. "We can do this."

And this time, the crack widened. Grasping the boards, I yanked, giving just enough room for my slender mother to slip through.

From the other side of the wall, she said, "I'll push, Darcy. Squeeze through."

Grunting, I maneuvered sideways through the opening. Never had I felt happier than I did at that moment, free from the dark and forbidding earth.

Slowly, my eyes adjusted to the anemic light filtering in. We didn't need the lantern any longer.

"Where in the world are we?" I whispered.

My mother actually clapped her hands. "I believe I know exactly where we are. Just look. It's no wonder we couldn't move those boards."

On the tunnel side, the partition had seemed to be a wall or a gate. On this side, those boards were the backdrop for shelves on which sat jars of canned vegetables and fruit. Several Mason jars lay broken on the floor, knocked off when we tugged the wall open.

Amazed, I muttered, "What in the world?" Mom laughed. "I do believe we are in a cellar."

She was right. Wooden shelves lined three walls containing the bounty of someone's garden. In front of us, six wood steps led to a slanting door. Cracks in the door let in the pale but beautiful light of day.

"Well, I don't care whose cellar it is. I just want out of here. I want to go home!" I started toward the steps.

"It's Ben's cellar," Mom declared, stopping me in my tracks. "It stands to reason if that cave was under his pasture and we were on his land. He must have covered the back wall with shelves to hide the opening into the hiding place for the gold."

Was Skye planning to show us the cellar when she came for a visit? She had said it was easier to show us the hiding place than tell us about it.

"Are you able to climb those steps and get out of here, Mom?" I asked.

She nodded. "I'll get up them if I have to crawl."

Setting the lantern on the floor, I started toward the stairs. I was standing on the second step with Mom behind me when the cellar door burst open and a large form barreled toward us, nearly knocking us over.

"Miss Darcy! Miss Flora! What are you doing here?" he yelled.

Mom caught her breath. "Jasper Harris! What under the sun?"

Peering up at this young giant towering over us, I felt neither shock nor surprise. After such an unbelievable day, I would not have been surprised to see anyone or anything. My mind and body felt numb.

We turned around and retraced our steps as Jasper clattered past us.

He seemed incredulous, staring first at my mother, then me. "Miss Darcy, you look awful. You've got blood and mud all over you and Miss Flora, your clothes are all torn and . . . why are you here? What are you doing messing around? Did somebody hurt you? How did you get down here? You shouldn't be here at all!"

Not wanting to take the time to explain to Jasper all that we had been through and wanting desperately to leave this underground room behind me, I shrugged.

Jasper's eyes narrowed. At last it must have dawned on him that we very likely knew far more about this place than anyone left alive, except himself. I could see the question coming before he asked it.

"Where did you come from? I mean, well, I don't mean that. Have you just been down here in the cellar or did you come from . . . ." He paused and glanced at the shelf-covered wall which stood partially open and the broken jars on the floor.

Mom interrupted. "If you are wondering whether we discovered your secret, Jasper, yes. We did. We know that Ben is back there. And we know the gold is there. Two killers are after us, bad men that want Ben's gold and they tried to kill us to get us out of the way. They chased us into the tunnel. Why did you bring Ben here? He should have been properly buried."

Jasper's face reminded me of a small boy who had just heard a story about monsters. "Killers?" he blustered. "Do you mean . . . are they the same ones who killed Mr. Ben?"

Sidling around us, Jasper edged toward the back wall. With a tug, he pulled it open. Lifting both hands, he turned to Mom and pleaded, "Miss Flora, you gotta believe me. I didn't know Ben was dead until I found him in the cemetery the day of the storm. I moved him 'cause I couldn't let him stay out in all that rain and hail. You understand, don't you?"

Mom spoke quietly. "Of course, Jasper."

"When you and Miss Darcy went into the chapel, the day of the storm, I slipped out the back. I had thought about what to do since I saw Ben out there on those sticks and rocks. I took him to the cave while you all were inside the chapel. I knew that Ben would want to be in that cave, but I sure couldn't tell the sheriff! He would've thought I killed Ben."

Jasper paused and wiped sweat from his forehead. "I found those rock steps by accident when I was noodling, and then I followed the tunnel on this side of the cave and came out here through Ben's cellar. Ben never did know that I found his secret. But I guess it ain't a secret no more. Now you all know about it and you know where Ben is."

Jasper looked as if he might start to cry.

Rubbing his hands through his hair, Jasper paced in a circle. "How did you all get out of the cave without setting off the trap?" he asked.

I grasped his arm. "What trap, Jasper?"

He shook me off. "Never mind. Now, I gotta think about this. What am I gonna do?"

Mom grabbed the front of his shirt. "Listen to me! We are all three going to walk out of this cellar, that's what we're going to do. Later, we'll sit down and figure out the whole thing. But right now, you are going to take us straight to your house so we can use the phone and call the sheriff and get Darcy to a doctor. We'll let the law handle this."

He shook his head. "No, I can't do that. The sheriff would find that gold back in there with Ben and he'd throw me in jail and . . . ."

Jasper's eyes swung toward the steps behind us just as a voice I had hoped never to hear again, said, "I don't think you'll have to worry about that, son."

Ray Drake jumped down the cellar steps. He wore a smirk and carried a gun that was pointing directly at us. His partner was at his heels. He too held a gun. My mother took two steps toward him, then put her arm around me.

"Hammer?" she whispered.

So, this was the second man, Ben's nephew. Or something more than a nephew? The man's dark good looks, the arched nose and chiseled face certainly reminded me of Ben.

For a few seconds, I felt as I had when I was ten years old and fell out of an apple tree flat on my back. My lungs seemed empty and I could not breathe.

How long had they been standing outside the cellar? Had they heard Jasper talking about the gold? Hammer's next statement answered that question.

"Just imagine finding you and Uncle Ben's gold all in the same day! So, that's where it is, back there!" He jerked his head toward the tunnel.

"And, to think, I've seen this cellar all my life and didn't know. I've hunted all over these hills, killed three stubborn people and, all along, it was right under my nose! My, my. Lady Luck is certainly smiling on me."

Mom's voice was deadly calm as she faced Hammer Ventris. "You murdered him. You murdered Ben, a man who always treated you fairly, had always been good to you. Then you murdered that antiques dealer in Oklahoma City and Skye. Poor little Skye, your own cousin. How could you do such cowardly, evil things?"

Hammer's eyes became black slits. "Cowardly? Evil? That depends on your line of thought. My thinking is that nobody ever wanted my mother or me. The Ventris family never let us forget that we owed them for the very food we ate. I'm going to take what I should have had in the first place. You see, Miss Flora, I knew that good ol' Ben had a soft spot for you. He wouldn't tell me where the gold was, no matter what

I threatened. Stubborn old man! But I figured he must have told you. I've been back in Ventris County for quite a while. You didn't know that I was anywhere near, did you?"

"You're right," Mom said. "I didn't know you were back in Ventris County. Last I heard, you were up north. I can't say much for the sort of friends you made there." She motioned in Drake's direction.

Ray Drake growled and started toward my mother. Before I could move, Jasper jumped in front of him. "Don't you hurt her!" he yelled. "She's a good woman."

"Aw, get out of my way, kid," Drake muttered. "I heard what you said about the gold. So, it's back in that tunnel there, is it?"

Jasper's face wore the petulant scowl of a child. "It ain't your gold. It's Mr. Ben's. You're not going to get your hands on it."

Drake laughed. "And who's going to stop me?"

"I am," I said. Not that I felt courageous. I just wanted to divert Drake's attention from Jasper who seemed to have no concept of guns and danger.

My ruse worked, probably all too well. Ray Drake turned that deadly looking barrel toward my mid-section. Grinning, he sneered, "Come on, then, if you're feeling brave."

I swallowed. At the moment, "brave" was not an accurate description of the way I felt.

While Drake's and Hammer's attention was on me, Jasper edged toward the back wall and the open doorway. Crossing my fingers, I hoped he could escape down that tunnel and bring help.

But, as he jumped through the opening, fruit jars fell and shattered. The two gunmen pivoted in his direction. Drake leveled a shot at Jasper, who disappeared in the darkness of the tunnel.

"Come back here, you dumb . . ." Drake yelled.

I felt frozen until I heard the sound of Jasper's feet growing fainter as he ran. Drake's shot had missed and I could breathe again.

Hammer turned back to his partner. "Stay here and watch these two. I'm going after that stupid kid!" He grinned and I felt goose bumps rise on my arms. "After I finish with him, I'll come back and take care of these two."

Drake's eyes turned toward Hammer. "Hey, stay away from that gold until we can count it out together!" he yelled.

Sometimes desperation spurs even the weakest creature to act irrationally. In the three seconds Drake's attention was on his partner, and with no doubt about what Hammer had in mind, I felt along the shelf behind me for a possible weapon. My probing fingers touched the cool, smooth sides of a heavy jar that Ben's wife probably canned years ago. Grasping the full jar, I swung my arm around, and hurled the missile at Drake's head.

It missed. The jar smacked Drake's hand and exploded. His gun flew across the cellar and slid along the floor toward me. I did not think; I reacted. Adrenalin surged through me and I lunged for the gun. Grabbing the weapon, I pointed it toward the man who had caused my mother and me such anguish.

The exploding jar had sprayed its contents all over Drake's face. He wiped peaches out of his eyes and glared at me. "That wasn't too smart. You know you're not going to shoot me," he muttered.

At that moment, fury gripped me such as I had never known. The cellar receded and all I could see was Drake's obnoxious grin, daring me to shoot.

"Just watch me," I said.

Mom's voice penetrated the haze. "Darcy!" she shouted. "Don't shoot! He's not worth it."

Drake sneered, "Sure, go ahead. You know you don't have the nerve." He started toward me.

At any moment, he would jump and grab the gun. Pointing the barrel in Drake's direction, I closed my eyes, and squeezed the trigger.

The gunshot, in that confined space, sounded like a cannon. The bullet hit the wall behind Drake, zinged across the room, and clinked into a shelf beside me. I hadn't considered a ricochet. For the space of half a dozen heartbeats, the three of us stood motionless.

Then, a big, black-looking blob appeared and spread across Drake's trouser leg, just above his knee. Staring at it, then at me, he croaked, "You shot me."

Evidently, the slug went through his leg before it bounced around the cellar. Glaring at me with pure hatred burning in his eyes, he slowly crumpled, like a disjointed puppet, to the floor.

Glancing at Mom, I expected to see her faint, but she astonished me. Her voice was strong as she said, "All right, he's not going to hurt us. Let's get out of here before that snake Hammer comes back." She plucked the gun from my suddenly limp fingers and slipped it into the pocket of her shirt.

"We are taking this with us," she said.

Turning our backs on Drake, who was screaming things no lady should ever hear, we hurried up the cellar steps to freedom. The feel of fresh, clean, moving air propelled me into the brightness of day-light. The rain had stopped at last and the sun had slipped toward the western horizon.

The longest day of my life was drawing to a close. I felt as if I had been underground for a week.

We paused on the cellar's top step. "Thank You, Lord," Mom whispered.

The spring day smiled innocently at us as if it knew nothing of storms or murderers or dead bodies. A raucous crow flew above the roof of Ben's red barn.

Mom pointed to an old, crumbling stone wall near the barn. "Let's get behind that fence," she said. "Hammer may come poking out of the cellar at any minute and, remember, he has a gun too."

We were halfway to the stone fence when the explosion came. A roar like a dozen freight trains crashed against my eardrums. The ground shook, an acrid smell filled the air, and it felt as if a giant hand pushed me to the earth.

Dazed, Mom and I stared at each other. "What happened?" I asked.

Slowly, I raised up on my knees and helped my mother from her prone position. A cloud of dust and smoke poured from the open cellar. Its door lay on the ground beside us. I watched, hypnotized as a yellow-black cloud drifted up into the sky and dissipated.

Like a gray ghost rising from the depths of the earth, a figure emerged from the cellar. It staggered toward us and flopped down at our feet.

"He bumped against the wire to my trap," Jasper said, gasping for air. "I didn't want to hurt nobody but anyhow, he won't bother you no more."

I put out my hand to touch Pat's dirt-covered son, just to be sure he was real. My voice sounded faintly over the ringing in my ears.

"He? Who, Jasper? Was it Hammer that set off your trap?"

Jasper nodded.

Mom scooted beside him. "And Drake? What about Drake?"

Jasper wiped grime off his face with his shirt sleeve. "He's still there in the cellar. He'll be there when Grant comes, I reckon. I knew Hammer was going to bump that wire. I yelled at him to stop but he shot at me. I started back to the cellar and the explosion happened and knocked me down."

An overwhelming weariness filled every muscle and bone of my body. I did not think I could move, even if I saw Drake and Hammer both coming at me.

"Your trap, Jasper, what kind of trap did you build?" I asked.

He breathed deeply and said, "I borrowed some dynamite from that ol' geezer that was damming the creek. I just took one stick and I wedged it in a crack close to that shelf that has the gold. I ran a wire from the stick and let it dangle above that wall that turns. I don't see how you all missed gettin' blown all to smithereens if you were around that turnin' wall."

Shaking my head, I admitted that I didn't understand either. But my mother did.

"God sent an angel to protect us," she said.

Somewhere down the road that led from Ben's place to town, came the wail of a patrol car. Or maybe it was an ambulance. Whichever it was, some worried neighbor must have heard the explosion and called the authorities. I was glad. It would be good to see Grant again. I wouldn't even mind if he yelled at me.

CHAPTER 26

I didn't remember much about the ride to Dr. McCauley's office nor Grant helping my mother and me into her house many hours later. The next day, I learned that both Pat and Jasper stayed the night with us. Pat made tomato soup and carried it to my bedroom and across the hall to Mom. Later, Pat told me that I drank that soup like I was starving, but I don't remember any of it. I do recall snuggling under warm blankets and the soft feel of my pillow under my head, but it was a feeling more than a memory. I slept until noon the next day.

When at last I awakened, I felt as if I had been kicked down the road and back by my neighbor's mule. Mom probably felt the same, although she never complained about her own aches and pains.

Easing my feet to the floor, I got out of bed and stumbled to the shower. The feel of warm water and the fragrance of soap washed away all lingering remnants of smoke and dirt from the day before. Everything except the memories was washed away. I had a feeling that the horror of my mother's and my flight through rain, briers, and an underground vault, plus the trauma of looking down the business end of a gun, and the terrible memory of that explosion would stay with me for a long, long time.

Drying off, I slipped on a gray, over-sized sweatshirt, a pair of my oldest and softest jeans, and stepped into warm, fuzzy blue house shoes. Pulling my damp hair into a ponytail, I glanced at my reflection in the mirror above the dressing table. I looked as if I had been fasting for a month. My cheeks were gaunt and shadows circled my eyes. My bangs only partially covered the stitches Dr. McCauley had put in my forehead, but I was alive. And so was Mom. Neither of us had broken bones or bullet holes.

"Thank you, Lord," I whispered. "You brought us through."

As I limped downstairs, I heard voices coming from the kitchen. Grant sat at the dining table watching Mom pour coffee into his cup. I marveled at how well she looked, wearing a perky red print dress and white apron. Her hair was fluffed into a halo around her face.

"Mom, are you all right? Shouldn't you be resting?" I asked, coming into the kitchen.

She smiled at me. "I feel as if a weight were lifted from my shoulders. Our long nightmare is over. Last night, I slept like a rock and today, I have more energy that I've had for a month. I'm glad to see you up, Darcy. Sit down and have some coffee and orange juice."

Grant rose and pulled out a chair for me at the table.

"Do you feel like answering a few questions?" he asked.

Direct and blunt, that was Grant Hendley. I knew these questions would be coming and I dreaded confessing my lack of honesty, but it would be a relief not to keep any more secrets.

The coffee was hot and strong and burned all the way down. Looking at Grant, I managed a smile. "Fire away," I said.

His blue eyes were as cold as gunmetal. "First of all, why didn't you tell me your plans for yesterday morning? The first inkling I had that you were not here at home was when a passer-by reported the broken guardrail on Deertrack Hill and the crushed undergrowth showing a car had gone over. Then, when Jim and I found your Passport and you and Miss Flora weren't anywhere around . . . ." He paused and gripped his coffee mug with both hands.

I reached across the table and touched his arm. "I tried to let you know Mom and I were leaving town; after all, you told us to go, if you'll remember. We were just following orders, but you didn't answer your phone. I'm truly sorry I didn't tell you what we knew about Jasper. He wouldn't go talk to you, Grant; he was afraid of jail. And now, I can see that he thought he had to keep Ben's secret, sort of loyalty to his friend. So Jim Clendon was with you when you found the Passport?"

He nodded. "Jim had been in Chicago, digging up information on Hammer and Drake. He just got back a couple of days ago."

So much for my suspicions, then. I wondered who chewed Red Man tobacco, Drake or Hammer?

Mom sat down with her coffee. "How's your head today, Darcy?" she asked.

"It doesn't hurt. My head is the hardest part of me, I suppose."

Grant snorted but, to his credit, he merely continued with his story.

"Jim found out that Hammer had gotten in with some big time bad guys in the windy city and wound up owing a lot of money in gambling debts. A crime boss set Drake on Hammer. That must have really put the fear into him and he remembered his uncle and the story about gold, so he came back to Levi and went to see Ben. I guess Hammer pestered him for a long time about that gold, but Ben was stubborn."

Mom ran her index finger around the rim of her cup. "That must have been what Ben meant when he said he thought something was going to happen to him."

Grant's mug banged against the table. "Ben Ventris told you that, Miss Flora? What else? I've known all along you two weren't telling me everything you knew about this case."

Taking a deep breath, I said, "Grant, I'm sorry. You're right. We shouldn't have kept all this from you. I hope we didn't break any laws. I'll tell you everything, but first—I have to know—did Hammer and Drake cook up this elaborate scheme between them, Drake pretending to be with the FBI and trying to scare us into telling him about the gold?"

"Well, what a relief that you're finally going to let me in on what you should have told me a long time ago," he said.

The sarcasm was back. Good. It was a shield against any tender emotions this man might evoke in my heart. At the moment, I wanted no romantic entanglements.

"Yes," Grant answered, "Hammer and Drake were in this scheme together and Hammer even engaged that high-priced lawyer, Rowley, thinking he could scare you into believing he had a legal right to Ben's treasure. Hammer will never have a chance to unburden his soul, but tough guy Drake is singing like a bird. I think his courage leaked out through that hole in his leg, Darcy."

Squirming in my chair, I closed my eyes against the memory of that awful time in the cellar. "So, is he going to be all right?"

Grant nodded. "Sure. Eventually. He asked for a guard outside his door because he's scared that some of his pals in Chicago might get to him before the law does. You were filling me in on your investigation, Darcy. I find it all very interesting."

Taking a deep breath, I began with Ben's will and Skye's letter and map. When I finished, thirty minutes later, I felt drained of the last dregs of energy. I had re-lived every excruciating moment. My hands shook as I lifted my coffee cup to my lips.

"I guess that's all, Grant," I said.

"And I guess that's enough," he muttered. Reaching for his Stetson on the chair beside him, he pushed away from the table.

"I'll go out this way, Miss Flora," he said, nodding toward the kitchen door. "Thanks for the coffee. I'll be in touch."

Shocked, I watched him go. Wasn't he going to say any more? I'd expected he would read the riot act to me and talk about the dangers of interfering with police matters or withholding evidence. He could at least have said, "Thank God you're safe." But he didn't. He just got up and left.

Mom and I looked at each other. She and I had lots to talk about too, but not today. Today was simply a time for recovery and a celebration of being alive.

CHAPTER 27

Birds sang in the thickets and a soft breeze brought the mysterious, elusive fragrance of the river. The sun felt warm on my shoulders. This lovely day stood out in sharp contrast to that day two weeks earlier when Mom and I started out in a thunderstorm to Fayetteville and wound up running for our lives. That terrible day marked an ending and a beginning. It answered the question of who killed three people and tried to kill two more, and it was the beginning of what I felt to be a new era in my life. I came back to my hometown of Levi like a wounded child running to its mother. My broken heart needed to mend and, in the strangest way, I felt that healing had begun. Grief over Jake's death was part of the past and I found myself looking forward to the future.

A vagrant breeze lifted my bangs off my forehead. The scar from the rearview mirror faded more each day. Dr. McCauley said that in time it would disappear. Maybe emotional wounds were like that. They grew fainter with time; that was a blessing.

My mother broke into my reverie. "Look at it, Darcy. Who would ever guess what lies beneath the surface?" Mom and I stood beside an indentation in the earth in Ben's pasture.

"No one would guess," I said, "except those of us who know."

Silently kneeling on the grass, she placed a bouquet of field flowers on the ground. I laid some daisies beside them. "For you, Ben," I said. "May you rest in peace."

Mom wiped her eyes. "Hammer too, Darcy. I hope he found some sort of peace. What a poor, tormented soul he must have been."

Strange that these two, the elder and younger Ventris, now shared a grave for eternity. Somehow, it seemed fitting, as if Ben's goodness might mitigate some of Hammer's evil.

Closing my eyes, I rejoiced once again at the simple pleasure of feeling the sun's warmth on my face. Under the serene beauty of this Oklahoma woodland, my mother and I experienced terror like we never could have imagined. I seemed unable to get enough fresh air, grass, bird song, and the joy of being alive.

Mom looked out across the hills. "I'm glad I had the cellar filled in," she said. "It was unsafe after the explosion. Besides, it was an entryway to a grave."

"Jasper's booby trap pretty much took care of the cave and everything in it. The way he had placed the explosive, the whole roof of the cavern collapsed and the tunnel just sort of folded in upon itself."

Slowly, Mom got to her feet. "What do you think Grant will do about Jasper?"

I stood up too. "Jasper may not have actually broken any laws except for . . . well, he did steal that dynamite, and I guess he may have had had evil intent when he rigged up the explosive to go off if anyone touched the wire. Of course, the explosion resulted in Hammer's death and, technically, Jasper caused it, but that could be construed as self-defense, seems to me."

"I imagine Grant will do his best to keep Jasper out of jail," Mom mused. "After all, what purpose would it serve to lock him up?"

We were walking back toward Mom's Toyota which was parked in Ben's driveway. "It wouldn't serve any purpose that I can see and would surely make him and Pat miserable. I still don't understand how we kept from setting off that explosion. We must have been a hair's breadth away from touching the trip wire."

"The Lord was taking care of us, Darcy," Mom said softly. "Don't you know that by now?"

Smiling at her, I said, "Yes, I believe I do. Before we go back home, do you feel strong enough to walk down to the creek?"

Mom stopped short, put her hands on her hips, and gazed at me. "I'm surprised that you want to go back there. Are you talking about that little ledge that marks the entrance to the tunnel and the gold?"

"Yes," I said. "I don't want to climb the bluff again; I just want to look at it."

Turning around, we headed in the opposite direction. It took only a few minutes to leave the grassy pasture and scramble down the rocky incline to the creek. Once again, water flowed through the channel. Grant took a court order to the rancher who had diverted the stream and told him to get rid of his dam.

Sitting down on a sun-warmed gray boulder, I looked up at the bluff that hid the back door to Ben's treasure trove.

"The ledge that jutted out over the tunnel is gone," I said. "Rocks and boulders have slid over it and completely hidden it. I can't see even a trace of the ledge nor the opening to the tunnel."

Mom lifted her shoulders. "I guess the explosion did that. Nobody could ever find that hole again, Darcy. It's covered by tons of rocks."

"Are you ever going to open it back up?" I asked. "There's an awful lot of gold under that hill."

She shook her head. "I doubt that I ever do anything more to this hillside. As far as I'm concerned, we are better off with the gold being buried with Ben and Hammer. I don't want any part of it. Ben didn't want the gold's hiding place exposed and I almost feel that it is cursed. It has certainly brought a lot of trouble."

Remembering the feeling I had when I held the beautifully wrought butterfly in my hand, I understood what she meant. The lure of gold could take over a person's life.

"There's a lot of people who know there's gold back in here somewhere. Do you think a thing like that can be kept secret? As soon as the good citizens of Ventris County realize you own all this and that legend of lost treasure is revived, you won't have a moment's peace," I said.

"It wasn't mentioned in the newspaper story about the explosion. Maybe people will just think it's gossip and interest will die down if we keep our mouths shut. Grant sure isn't going to say anything. By the way, Darcy, he isn't too happy with us, you know."

I grinned. "That's an understatement. I've told him I'm sorry that I didn't keep him posted on what was going on with us. And I've asked the Lord to forgive me for lying and for shooting that awful Ray Drake or Cub or whoever he is."

"But Darcy," Mom said, "you didn't have a choice. He was going to kill us."

"I know, but more than that was the way I felt when I shot that horrible man. I hated him, Mom. Maybe I shot him because I hated him, not because I feared for our lives. I don't know."

Mom patted my knee. "You did what you had to do. The Lord knows your heart better than you do."

Looking up at the ruined bluff, I said, "Well, yes, but I wish my heart had purer motives. Remember what Emma James said about temptation hitting us when we are weak? I had felt criticism toward Ben at the thought that he might have had a relationship with Hammer's mother, but I guess I was feeling a little superior, a little 'holier than thou.' I discovered I could actually shoot another human being, and that emotion I felt—the hatred—is what I needed to have forgiven."

Something on the ground glittered in the sunlight and I bent to pick it up. The gold circlet that nestled in my palm was a larger edition of Mom's ring. I stared at it for a moment, then gently opened her hand and laid the ring in it.

She gasped. "Why, Darcy! This is Ben's ring."

"Yes," I said. "Hammer must have lost it when he and Drake were chasing us."

She closed her fingers around the ring and held it against her face. "I'll keep it with mine in the recipe box," she said.

Blinking tears from my eyes, I gazed at these hills surrounding us. They had witnessed much through the centuries. If they could talk, what stories they would tell of love, heroism, frailties, greed, and hope. And one day, perhaps the story of Ben and Hammer and the gold, and even Mom and I, would become part of the folklore for future generations.

At last, Mom spoke quietly. "I've been thinking about what Hammer said there in the cellar, about feeling unloved and being resentful. I've been thinking about Ben's farm and how it could be turned into a home for children who need fathers and mothers to care for them. Maybe the farm could be a place where orphans learn about work and honesty and God's love. The farm is a good place, Darcy. There's the creek for fishing and swimming, there's wood to chop for the fireplace, and Ben had a wonderful orchard back behind his house."

I grinned at her. "So you're planning on making something good come out of all that has happened." I should have known that Flora Tucker would not want to profit from Ben's estate.

"Does that sound all right to you?" Mom asked.

Nodding, I said, "It most certainly sounds wonderful."

A movement above me caught my eye and I looked up as a great owl swooped through the air and landed on the low branch of a sycamore. Cocking its head toward us, it called softly.

My breath caught in my throat. Why had this shy, nocturnal bird lit so close? As I gazed, it lifted its wings as if pronouncing a benediction, then flew silently into the woods, through a dark canopy of trees, and out of sight.

I felt blessed. Tragedy had touched the lives of my mother and me, but God had brought us through. Getting to my feet, I reached down a hand to Mom.

"Do you know what I'd like now, above all else?" I asked.

"No, Darcy Tucker Campbell, what would you like above all else?" Mom teased.

"I'd like a cup of your famous brew, perked in that old yellow coffeepot, so strong that a spoon could stand alone in it. I want to sit at your dining table with the sunlight coming through your west window and think of nothing else in the whole world except that you make the best caffeine in all of Ventris County."

"Only in the county? Who else in Oklahoma can brew a better cup?" she asked.

Laughing, I said, "Nobody, Mom. Nobody else in the whole Sooner state."

— THE END —

About the Authors

It may seem strange to some that a mild-mannered kindergarten teacher would become an author of cozy mysteries, but it's actually a good fit. A teacher is a word craft. So is a writer. A teacher wants the efforts of her labor to have a positive outcome. So does a writer. A teacher prays and hopes that each student has a positive take-away from her work. A writer hopes that for her readers too. A teacher would like each of the children in her classroom to achieve a satisfying life. Although she can't control that, as a writer she can control the way her books conclude!

A native Oklahoman, Blanche has a deep familiarity with the Sooner state, so it's the logical setting for her books. Her Cherokee heritage and feeling at home in the rural settings of Oklahoma are vividly woven into the background fabric of her books. Her other published cozies include *Grave Shift* and *Best Left Buried*, books two and three on the Flora/Darcy Series, co-authored by Barbara Burgess.

Barbara Burgess is a retired trial court administrator who says she found many good story ideas in the courtroom. One of those ideas evolved into her first suspense novel, *Lethal Justice*, published in 2010. She also co-authored *The Cemetery Club*, a mystery novel based on Cherokee history. Her father was half Cherokee and she says much of her family history involves Cherokee legend and beliefs similar to those found in *Grave Shift*. She has also written short fiction for *Woman's World* and Alfred Hitchcock's *Mystery Magazine* and freelanced for several Arkansas newspapers.